The Ports

Collected Stor

By
Michael W. Thomas

Black Pear Press

The Portswick Imp
Collected Stories: 2001 - 2016
By
Michael W. Thomas

First published in April 2018 by Black Pear Press
www.blackpear.net

ISBN 978-1-910322-57-4

Front cover artwork by Ted Eames
Cover design by Black Pear Press
Edited by Black Pear Press
Additional proofreading by Katherine Dixson

Dedication

To Lynda

Acknowledgements

Most of the stories have appeared in the following magazines, whose editors Black Pear Press and Michael W. Thomas would like to thank: *Under the Radar, Staple New Writing, Theaker's Quarterly Fiction, Gold Dust Magazine, Etchings (Australia), The Interpreter's House, Muscadine Lines (US), The Antioch Review (US)*.

'Catching the Light' was Shortlisted and Highly Commended for the George Orwell Dystopian Fiction Prize, 2017.

Contents

Strawberries And Frightened Water

It was hot. Everyone agreed that the stage got smaller every year. Suggestions were rife: get a few fans up there, arrange the chairs differently, let some staff sit at the back of the hall. But nothing changed. A particular Friday in July impelled sixty-odd bodies to meld in sufferance, becoming a beast which sighed from its many mouths, rubbed its weary legs.

This year, the end of term speaker was a biggish noise in education consultancy. He stalked his portion of the stage, praising this initiative, drubbing that government plan. To his left, the Headmistress followed his moves with an interest that was beginning to sour. None of the staff could catch much of what he said. At one point, he threw a sheaf of papers to the floor, and the composite beast behind him rippled with shock. Even the Headmistress leaned forward, abandoning her attempt to remember the name of Paul Newman's last film. But then there came a tide of mainly girlish mirth from the well of the hall. His eruption had been scripted; the rows and rows of pupils and parents, or clients and their backers, were laughing with, not at him.

On the back row of the stage, Jane Pearson studied the nape of Matthew Tate's neck. It was more attractive close up. She'd thought exactly that the previous night, as always, while he arched his back and she did that particular thing he liked. Smooth as anything his nape was: a gift of creamy skin, to compensate perhaps for the untimely wrinkles elsewhere. Not a bad body, but capable of unappealing surprises—scrawniness, for

1

example, where there should be generosity.

A line from a Martial epigram, cheerfully coarse, pushed into her thoughts, and she looked around to see if anyone had heard her groan. The first two days of the holidays would be shot with those damn subject meetings. Out of the blue, her Department Head had decided to ditch the current Latin A-level syllabus and go for something new—and experimental, if you please. Jane couldn't believe it. The woman was usually a millpond. Change, she'd often claimed, was something that airy-fairy subjects went in for: Economics, IT. But now, Jane and the others would have to spend all summer battling with stuff they hadn't taught for ages— the loathsome Martial included.

Another of his epigrams, appallingly ripe, filled her mind. Jane tried to give it the slip but realised that she had nothing good to think about. Again she stared at Matthew Tate's neck, now willing it to erupt in boils. He'd let her do what she did last night, every last rub and lick, before telling her. The cheek of it…the everything of it! 'No, she's moved on to pastures new,' he'd assured Jane again and again. 'Good and gone, she is.'

At the front of the stage, the speaker was now lurching about, jiggling an official report in the air as though it were a bone to entice an origami dog. Several people were laughing. Make them stop, thought Rhoda Willersley—please. The man's a buffoon. Even by the usual end-of-year standards, he's beyond dreadful. And that jiggling was giving her a headache…well, worsening the one she had. Again she cursed her ill luck in being parked on the front row. The likes of Jane Pearson, they had the right idea. In fact, she'd been right behind Jane when they all came onto the stage—confident that, for once, the anonymity of the back row would be hers. But then things had gone twisty and broken up, as they sometimes did. The next thing she knew, some well-meaning clown was chaperoning her to this seat, the last one left. There was nowhere for her eyes to go. If she looked down into the hall, the regiment of stares made her feel naked, soiled. If she looked at the buffoon, her head split a little more.

Cautiously, her tongue investigated her mouth. Dry as a desert. It wouldn't be—not if she hadn't made that mistake. But no, it wasn't a mistake. She knew she'd put it there: a new place, to be on the safe side. Nearly full, too, with one of those fiddly caps. Better a fiddly cap, though, than any loss of life. That's how she'd always seen it, whatever colour it was, whatever provenance, however cheap. Life, pure and simple, never mind the taste. She'd gone for a needed top-up just before the bell dragged everyone to the hall. But it had vanished: not in the document box, not behind the shelf. Someone must have known. Just her luck, someone picking that moment to show concern. Or be a vicious cow.

The speaker was swinging this way and that, raking the air with his hands. Just behind Rhoda Willersley, Eleanor Laird was all alarm. What was the man doing? Inviting the entire stage to scrum down with him? Gearing up for a cringeworthy pirouette? But then he called a name, and Tom Howsell sprang up at the end of her row. Amid applause, and some over-appreciative cries from the girls, he joined the speaker for handshakes and the bestowal of a certificate. Oh my, thought Eleanor. So Tom got the teaching award after all. So no one found out. So I'm the keeper of his secret and he doesn't even know.

Yet again, she pictured the Reception room at the front of the school, its handsome drapes and carpeting. A bit dishevelled, it was, after that Sixth Form debate. The cleaners would have their work cut out next morning; she remembered thinking so as she'd hurried back for her forgotten pile of books. She'd nearly decided that they would keep, only to be ambushed by her librarian self, the one who ticked the girls off for their cavalier attitude to her precious stocks. Oh, she'd imagined the chanting: Lairdy's lost her books! Lairdy the Loser!

There'd been no-one in the Reception room—so she thought, till, with the recovered books in her hand, she'd turned for the door. But one of the drapes had squawked and billowed aside, revealing Tom Howsell and…whatever her name was—one Upper Sixth blonde looked just like the next. Not that Eleanor had got the best view of her: Tom's back, yes, broad and half-shirtless. But the girl…Eleanor's life had not been without adventure, was occasionally colourful still, but she couldn't believe that one human being could bend another quite like that. The girl was a rubber doll beneath him. Above and around him, too.

The applause was still going strong as Tom Howsell resumed his seat. Eleanor scanned the audience to see if she could spot the girl—or at least a pair of hands clapping extra hard beneath that just-had-sex hairstyle

4

they were always being told off about. But she abandoned the search as another memory got in front of Tom and the girl and the drapes. 'Well, Eleanor,' came the Headmistress's crisp, girlish voice. 'We've appointed Polly. She'll be such a boon for you.' Yes, thought Eleanor now. Polly the computer whiz. Polly the doyenne of library systems. Something a touch lopsided about her. Smile just a bit too big for her face. But there—usurpers come in all shapes and sizes.

Now the Headmistress rose to thank the speaker. Jane tried and failed to catch his name. In her mind, Matthew Tate's neck was scabrous and wasted. I'll go over tonight, she thought. I'll have it out with him and that wife-who-wasn't-but-is-again, if she's there. What were they planning? Re-marriage? Or had they never—? The enormity of the thought almost caused Jane to slide off her chair. He'd never actually said 'divorced'—she'd just assumed, and he'd let her. On the other hand—this time she did slide a little—she'd never so much as seen a photo of the woman. Did she exist? Was this a ploy of his—a regular one? Tate's Patent Girlfriend Remover? All Threats of Commitment Erased? Before she knew it, her hand was reaching out to him. Only at the last second did she turn vengeance into a stretch. I'll go over, she thought. I'll bring down his roof.

Only minutes to go, thought Rhoda as the Headmistress wrapped up her little speech. Thank God the buffoon had put his papers down—much more jiggling and she'd have blacked out. Now for the bunfight on the lawn. Soggy strawberries, tasteless cream. Before all that, though, she'd go hunting for her lifeline again. She was sure she'd put it there—she could remember the way the glass chinked against the side of that shelf. The wine on offer outside would be less than useless—just frightened water, really. It sure as hell wouldn't protect her against the Huskissons.

They'd know the moment she stepped into the sunlight. It was cruel, really: Mrs H always wore something terrifying on her head, some get-up from a malarial vision of Ascot—she was easy to spot across any stretch of grass in England. Yet even with that warning, Rhoda could never escape. Mrs could dip and weave; so could Mr. As often as not, Rhoda would turn to flee, only to bounce off his rubberised belly. Then they'd have her, and the talk about 'our spirited Gemma' would come thick and fast. Spirited, yes. If Social Services ever touched the world of the Huskissons, they'd have to work in relays to deal with that spirit. Gemma would be starting her GCSEs next year. Rhoda just knew she'd be saddled with her for History—none of her colleagues would touch her. The Huskissons would know, too, without being told. They'd stare intently at Rhoda as their interrogation droned on. Rhoda would have to drum up grace under fire—principally from the wayward lunges of whatever perched atop Mrs's head. Their eyes would narrow; they'd scrutinise her for signs of unsteadiness. Mrs might comment airily on some news item she'd read about the official dispatch of some unfit teacher. Mr would assure Rhoda—and everyone within thirty yards—how much he was looking forward to another year on the Board of Governors. Rising to depart with the rest of her row,

6

Rhoda wondered whether she shouldn't just grab a bottle of the godawful wine and quit school and town forever.

Shouldering a space for herself in the lines exiting the hall, Eleanor nearly bumped against a now familiar sweater. She prayed that its owner wouldn't turn round. Ah, hello Polly, she'd have to say, then nod idiotically as the woman ran through, yet again, the stuff they'd be discussing in the library next week. Yes, Polly knew what was what—databases, systems, innovations in cataloguing. One of those memory stickies swung permanently from her flawless neck. Pushed along in the flow, Eleanor imagined a conversation a year from now, out on the lawn: the Headmistress, pressured from above, speaking not unkindly about budgets and restructuring, asking what Eleanor thought about going half-time, or less, or even… No immediate rush, the Headmistress would say a year from now. Think about it. Enjoy the summer. Eleanor saw Tom Howsell up ahead. Well, if she was going anyway, soon or late… She imagined leaping on him: 'The drapes, Tom,' she'd cry. 'Bend me, bend me.'

The lines broke on the steps to the lawn. Jane found herself with Eleanor on one side and Rhoda, her mouth still dry, on the other. Down in the ruck, Matthew Tate cackled; a nightmare of ribbons and silk bobbed above random groups; Polly laid a hand on the arm of a smitten father. The three women stood like explorers with toes flush against the first yard of a desert. Well, well, said one of them as they stared at the blank mass of summer that waited beyond the lawn. As if with hands joined on a dare, they stepped together.

First published in *Muscadine Lines: A Southern Journal #33—January-March 2011*

Catching The Light

Martin Finch stared through the window of the only shop in Harbours Hill. It was late afternoon but autumn had come with winter on its back so it felt like night. The shop had been one of those convenience stores such as you once found at large petrol stations, with maybe a drinks counter and a few tables. One-stops, they used to be called. This was certainly a one-stop now. All sorts were piled up, almost to the ceiling in places.

The shop was bright. Storm-lamps hung here and there. Heavy-duty models, thought Martin, wondering where they'd come from. Rare as hens' teeth now, or at least that size was. Of course, a lot of people had got stuff in good time or, answering an atavistic prompt to make do and mend, had never thrown it away. He'd done neither. Even so, he made out all right: fettling unused floor tiles to cover the wind-blown patches on the roof, finding that home-brew kit in the cellar and refashioning the barrels, with almost unused sealant, into a decent bowser. His wife and daughter couldn't complain. Not on those scores, anyway.

The brooch was right by the window, stuck to the lapel of a man's jacket, next to a few peg-bags with plastic clips. Screws and nails in those, he guessed: small salvage. The lamplight was drawn to the brooch, inflaming the pattern picked out in its coloured glass. Could be diamonds—even, as they used to say, priceless. Entirely safe, now, to leave diamonds unattended in a lamp-lit shop in a dark village. These days priceless simply meant what it said. Wine-red, the pattern was: a rose in full bloom. Martin fancied that, in real life, a rose like that would have taken its time to unfurl, ignoring its sun-thirsty neighbours.

'Something nice,' Sarah had idly said. 'Something to set among the candles.' She'd had no clear idea in mind and her musings hadn't sent him out now. His daughter had always loved candles, even as a little girl. She used to love lighting them then turning the lights off to watch them stretch and flicker. Now that that was pretty much all they had (he really should hunt up a good storm-lamp), she wanted to trick them out, titivate the glow. She used to make her own—still did on the odd occasions when she'd scavenged enough wax.

'Bloody idiocy,' Simon would say. 'The more people do that, the less chance there is they'll get the electrics going regular.' A chancer himself, her husband: long gone now, in the dead of night, probably to try his luck on one of the freedom-boats. They were free, all right, free to get nowhere. Just last week someone came through Harbours Hill telling of a boat turned back between Guernsey and St Malo. It was much the same in all directions and sometimes worse: heavy shelling from the Wexford coast, bombers dispatched from Reykjavik to dissuade a boat rounding the Faroe Islands.

That'd do it, thought Martin, watching how the brooch seemed to pulse in the faint swing of a storm-lamp. That'd go with the candles. He went in, pushing his way past several squinters and rummagers.

'Ah, Finch.' Lord Hunnington managed a smile. His smile came almost naturally these days as he stood with hands spread on the counter, though he hadn't, probably wouldn't, lose the habit of surnames alone. Hunnington Hall was no longer his, save for a few rooms in one wing, where his many children, permanently home from defunct boarding-schools, were reputedly turning feral. It had been requisitioned by Birmingham Council, or what was left of them, once the looters, lead-thieves and IT bandits had reduced their offices in Victoria Square to the point of no return. Now about thirty people rattled around in most of Hunnington Hall, ineffectually stabbing the keyboards of a few computers during the daily two hours of official mains time and trying to sustain the notion that England was unbowed. As for Lord Hunnington, his forebears had been wool barons and, needing to get away from his young savages, he had uncovered a modest entrepreneurial flair. The shop had been a post office and was therefore no longer of use, so he'd taken it over as a commodity-hub. Atavism again, thought Martin.

'So then,' he said now, 'what has waylaid your fancy?'

'In the window. That brooch among—'

A sharp toot interrupted them, as of a kazoo with a sense of destiny. Everyone in the shop turned and looked at the shelf behind Lord Hunnington's head. From a wind-up radio issued the latest announcement. There were only two stations now. One was a plunder of the archives. Once more, Cliff Michelmore and Jean Metcalfe played records for British forces dispatched across a still-pinkish map; Mrs Mopp asked Tommy Handley if she could do him now; and a jingle of more recent origin sang of 'Kenny Everett and Chris Denning, both together on the wireless machine.' The other station, possibly live, was devoted to Brains Trust-style debates, bulletins about the state of the nation and updates on efforts to get it back on track. The boisterous kazoo meant a bulletin. Habit, Martin guessed, made everyone stop and turn. Someone from whatever passed for the Government began speaking, as so often before, of misunderstanding, ill-judged words spoken in the heat of some long-gone moment, new initiatives in train 'with our fellow nations to north, south, east and west.' The fare on this station was even more monotonous than the Huggetts and the Clitheroe Kid. At the mention of official initiatives, everyone always went back to what they were doing. In the shop they did so now.

'Ah,' said Lord Hunnington, 'the brooch. Only happened on it this morning.' His eyes misted a little. 'My great-grandmother's. Presented to her by Queen Alexandra, did you know that?'

Martin smiled at *did you know that?*—a relic itself of the time when the Lord Hunningtons of the world confidently assumed that everyone was up to speed, or should be, with the minutiae of noble houses.

'Anyway,' he went on, 'hardly much use in what they have long been pleased to call the new reality. Sad but true. Can't loiter for sentiment, Finch.' He closed his eyes against the hint of a tear. 'But it must go to a good home. That is'—he rubbed thumb and forefinger together—'an understanding home.' With these last words he leaned over the counter and tilted his head.

Martin's commodity-bag was full. Not a bad haul in the last week. He'd learnt how to avoid the North Worcestershire gangs, who in any case were notoriously

12

unmethodical, leaving pickings for the careful slipper-and-slider. To begin with, of course, it had been different; his left shoulder still gave him grief from that encounter in the house at Dunhampton. But the gangs knew to avoid the commodity-hubs, whose proprietors were without exception on the ball. In a cupboard behind Lord Hunnington were three twelve-bore shotguns, all loaded. Rarities themselves now: miraculously, when the change had begun and gangs had just started forming, all ammunition had been buried, locked or otherwise removed from their way, leaving them to eke out what they had. (There was no hope of replenishment: underworld suppliers were forensically located.) It was arguably the last act of a coherent society. Worries soon arose, of course, about break-outs from the faltering prisons, the risk that seasoned professionals would swell the gangs' ranks. The decision taken in respect of all prisoners, however young, was the first act of a society fated to be very different.

'My word,' breathed Lord Hunnington as they leaned towards each other to screen the items from view. 'Go on, Finch, get it, quick.' When Martin returned with the brooch, Lord Hunnington was covertly turning the two packets round and round below the counter. 'Thought all these had gone. Even the e-brands. My word. Pall Malls.' He grinned broadly. 'I'll ration one pack for my troglodytes. Give 'em a taste of the old glory days.' He stroked his chin. 'I've heard tell again of a wacky-baccy outfit somewhere up towards Quinton. If I can get some, I'll mix it in with these. Shut the little buggers up for hours on end.'

13

'Sounds like a plan,' said Martin and both of them laughed. The notion of a plan was now as ghostly as the voice of Jean Metcalfe as she prepared to spin Slim Whitman's latest for a soldier in Aden.

Leaving the shop, Martin thought of Richard and, as always, wondered where he was. The last time Martin saw him, he was at the other end of a very long line. The last he knew for definite, he was part of a dig in Queensland. Well, he'd been with him then. It had been a toss-up between him and his wife to go out and visit their past-obsessed son. Or not so much that: Andrea hadn't been keen on the idea of a long-haul flight, preferring to wonder aloud—and via Skype to Richard—why there weren't suitable projects closer to home. When she'd been asked to do extended cover at work, the trip fell to him.

He hadn't exactly jumped at it. He wanted to see Richard properly, released from a Skype-screen, but the prospect of the flight hadn't chuffed him either. Once he was there, of course, Andrea changed her mind, rejigged things at work and was well along with preparations to join them. Then she wasn't. Martin had only been out there about a week when the news from home started breaking.

At first, it seemed like some routine kerfuffle: international court finds fault with how a country does this and that, lots of agitated straplines running along the bottom of bulletin-screens, soothing words from a Grand Poobah representing the country in question, normal service resumed. It soon became clear that this was different. An ambassador said something, which was suavely denied; a consul insisted on something else, which was denied with heat; an international spokesman trashed the denials and was doused in expletives. All over London and other British cities, embassies, consulates and missions shut up shop. The Australian news bulletins particularly favoured a clip of the Norwegian ambassador quitting Belgrave Square, getting his shoulder-bag caught in the gates and punching a policeman who tried to assist.

But hard facts were impossible to come by. Why was this happening? What had Britain done? Soon a global deportation of British nationals was underway: 'a Pommy-shit', as Queenslanders cheerily called it. UK planes were allowed to touch down on all the airstrips of the earth—and grudgingly refuelled—to get every last Brit off foreign soil. With scores of others, Martin was herded into the belly of an ex-Oxfam cargo plane in Brisbane and dispatched to Hong Kong, where they were allowed to jostle around in a high-walled freight yard for a couple of hours until the second leg. The plane landed at Brize Norton at some ungodly hour and after that it was every man, woman and child for themselves. A few of them had been taken ill on extended holidays and, no treatment forthcoming, died en route. On both planes, Martin and the other passengers kept trying to get an explanation but were just told to sit still and shut up. Once he was threatened with a pistol-butt.

At least, once back, he only needed to thumb two rides, Brize Norton to Malvern, Malvern to home. The first was a lorry carrying supplies for something called a security-hub in Guarlford. (He was soon to discover that 'hub' was appended to every organisational gesture and that, as with 'plan', its meaning was pretty shaky.) The driver and his mate were sanguine about the state and future of the country:

'These things, they happen,' said the driver, making it sound like a protracted tiff. 'They'll sort it out. We've been through worse.' Complementing this faith in authority's vision, the mate execrated every soul living beyond Dover. Martin had been going to ask them for details of what had happened. He decided against. But he did ask the doctor who, edging carefully round the lakes of glass from a looted retail park, pulled up for him in Malvern Link. The back of the doctor's car was packed out: suitcase, cardboard boxes, plastic bags full of packets, tubes, syringes. Wellbeing hubs, he said: all general practitioners had been ordered to leave their surgeries, take what supplies they had to hand and join huge teams in hastily-converted warehouses and supermarkets. His hub (a slow smile at the word) was up in Rowley Regis.

Not that Martin got an answer straight off. The doctor was far more interested in him. 'Queensland, eh?' he asked, threading his way along the South Worcester by-pass, past cars joy-ridden out of fuel. 'Shame you couldn't vanish.'

'They made sure we didn't,' said Martin and Richard's face filled his mind. He'd follow on, he told his dad: just a thing or two to sort out at the dig and then a colleague would drive him to Brisbane airport. So he arrived late…well, he was always late, one of the lovable and maddening things about him. Then again, the dig was some two hundred miles north. Stepping out of the embarkation line, Martin had finally spotted him at the

16

far end: combat pants, puffer-jacket, that bush-hat with the bird-of-paradise feather that made him look like a Restoration rake. See you on board, Richard's wave had said. Once up the steps, Martin had squashed himself to one side to wait, but a soldier manhandled him to a strap-seat at the far end. He craned around for Richard but the cabin was long and barely lit. During the two hours in Hong Kong, he combed the freight-yard: no sign. Well, Richard had the knack of friendship. It wasn't impossible that someone—the nameless colleague? an official, even?—had ensured that he was marked on the list and then spirited him up to Rockhampton, back out to the Blackwater country, letting him melt away.

Blinking, he found that they were on the M5, heading for the Kidderminster exit, and the doctor was talking about cholera:

'It'll be back. They all will, dysentery, the works. What I've got in the back is just about it for me. Same with all my colleagues. Oh, we've been promised fresh supplies…probably courtesy of flaky websites, gangsters from all points of the compass. God, the way they think of this country now, all we'll get are Dignitas kits.'

On the exit slip they slowed down. An ancient police car was parked on the verge, its blue light perched drunkenly on the side of the roof. Reaching down, the doctor produced a sign saying *Medic* and pushed it against the windscreen. A bandaged hand waved them on. Staring a moment at the sign, the doctor snorted and dropped it into his foot-well. Finally, Martin asked him.

'What happened?' The doctor shrugged. 'Maybe what was bound to happen. This country hobbled the future of others often enough. Now they've done likewise.' He rubbed his chin. 'Not a planned thing, as far as anyone can tell, and nothing to do with all that EU referendum malarkey a few years back. More like'—he biffed the wheel—'international telepathy.' He considered what he'd just said. 'A global salmon run, if you see what I mean.'

Martin said he did.

'Of course our leaders blustered, then got riled, then effed and cussed. You'll hear 'em at it on the radio—by the way, try and hunt down all the small batteries you can find—and you'll hear 'em saying that the rest of the world will come to its senses and we'll'—another snort— 'gather lilacs in the spring again.'

'You don't think so?'

'I've come to believe that countries have their allotted time. I don't mean invasions or fiddling with borders. They just have to die. Anyway, all the rest, they've got their own copies of Jane Austen, the Beatles, Monty Python. Freetown, Sri Lanka, Helsinki…someone'll be putting a Shakespeare on. They've got the knack of football and the web.' He grinned at Martin. 'We've done our nice and nasty bit. And now, here we are.'

Stumbling, Martin steadied himself against a tree. He kept forgetting about the roots pushing through the path just there. Fine thing if he were to fall and crack his skull open just yards from home. Turning, he looked back down at Harbours Hill: one or two lights were still flickering, a slither of metal said that Lord Hunnington was securing his commodity-hub for the night. Another sound made him tense: no, just a cat, a fox, rather than a snot-nosed novice hoping to win his gang spurs with a first assault. After discovering the brooch, he didn't want to end the day with his other shoulder done in.

The brooch. Taking it from his commodity-bag, he turned it over in his hand. Even in the darkness it seemed to give a faint gleam, as though tuned to the last signal from a long-dead star. Sarah would love it. Watching how it answered light for light with the candles would carry her through the evening—him, too, and Andrea. Of course, there was big, wide, messy tomorrow to deal with, more scavenging, more self-righteous vituperation from the airwaves, more need to curl his fingers round the knife deep in his pocket, just in case.

Here we are, he thought, echoing the doctor's final words. But somewhere out there was Richard. For a long while Martin had been angry and sad; Andrea had stayed silent. But his feelings changed, as, in time, did hers. Why shouldn't he have a shot at freedom? Wouldn't they have done the same in his place, at his age? He rather thought they would.

Picking his way to the gate, he pictured his son: on a veranda in the Blackwater country, maybe, or much further in, protected, doing a fine Aussie accent, laughing, hopeful…

Shortlisted & Highly Commended: *Orwell Society Dystopian Fiction Prize, 2017*

Phyll And Fog

1.

Run. Run down all the Americas. Find what waits. Square up. Do what you can't help. You too. Follow. Seek and hide. Feel fear, feel wonder. Beauty awaits! Triumph awaits!

I could have been an historian. Properly. A contending voice in the pages of journals that matter. I could have run a B&B in Nether Stowey. Stowey. Stowaway. Out of sight, nothing to pull aside the leaves of my world. I could have done both. I can organise, I can feel my way round time. The landlady-historian: that would have got attention—of the shallower kind to start with, no doubt, but I could have made that work for me. Is it a historian? An historian? I've never known. That's precisely the kind of worry that stopped me going there. To proper history. To Nether Stowey. I always see a little ball of fluff with a whistle twice its size, tooting in the silence. That's how worry goes. So—teacher-training instead and, Lord, it was desperate. Who were those people with their folders and colour-codes? What came after was worse. Then it was wonderful. And now, God help me, it's this.

2.

Coarsely she complained, calling them the work of nutters. Even so, Phyllis Erika Welford lived with the sentiments in her school reports. This was just as well, for, in her five years at Belvoir School, those sentiments followed her tirelessly about. Belvoir School prided itself on how it tagged its girls' development. When new index-systems were devised, Belvoir set its shield and Latin at their head. When spreadsheets appeared—and, in time, someone who understood them—those same trademarks wavered on a computer screen's margin. None of this, however, could capture the likes of Phyllis.

Still, she progressed in her way. Seasons changed, and she graduated from *indifferent* through *sullen* to *fractious*. *Negative* always lurked somewhere, a mother encouraging her brood. Mathematically able, except when asked to be, Phyllis once gathered all her reports together, graphing the increase in *negative* from her first year to her fourth. The curve rose entrancingly to the top right-hand corner. Phyllis at eleven was 42% *negative*; by fifteen, she was romping home with 87. She laughed at this: no, cackled, like a witch in *Macbeth* who had weirder doings in hand than bamboozling a thane. She was her cackle.

She soon disposed of 'Phyllis', regarding herself as sharp, knowing—as Phyll. One hastily cancelled report dissented, preferring *a lump of lard*. And there was something lardy in the sight of her up at a boarding-house window, barracking the comprehensive kids who passed below, mad for a response in kind, even a venomous look. When she got either, her eyes would mist like a toper's. Then some elder would arrive, dressing her down, sometimes attempting Belvoir's motto. Phyll would roll away from the sill, choose *sullen, confrontational* or another mood officially inscribed for her and depart, cackle brewing.

Gets it from her parents: that was the explanation fixed on by a school to which she gave nothing away. It sounded plausible. Dumping her on Belvoir betrayed her

21

parents' idea of where duty ended. She was a blot on their picture of ease. Educationally, she was a child of limbo, since they didn't want her to stay on for the Sixth Form at Belvoir or go anywhere else. The mother was shrewish, quick to hint a belligerence that never quite surfaced. The father wasn't anything, present in body alone at parents' meetings, and then only fitfully since he was forever nipping out for a smoke. His mind was two hundred miles away, among the copious plans and loud phone calls of his *des res* construction company. Yet *gets it from her parents* wasn't enough. The mother's manner wasn't Phyll's, nor was the father's indifference. She'd become what she was when they weren't looking, and since they so rarely looked, there'd been a lot of time for the unfathomable to form behind her eyes.

That freckle. It was on the edge of her right cheekbone, far from the cluster round her nose. The other cheek was clear. At first I thought it was a mole, a neglected dab of ink. It always appeared at the edge of my sight. Edges: my sight, her cheekbone. Like for like. I'd be talking to a group of younger ones in Long Hallway, or calming an Oxbridge hopeful outside the History Room. And up it swam, Welford's freckle, like a flake of dirty snow. Then her whole cheek, her whole face. Out of nowhere. She could have been in the gym a moment before, or skiving in town, but somehow she knew that I was in a corridor, in open country.

She preferred it when I had a group around me. She liked to slide in at the back like a film extra: *baffled villager, jostler at public meeting.* And she'd get my whole attention:

22

it wasn't mine to keep. The ones in front of her, beaming or fretful, they'd just melt. I'd be left with her and a mass of shadows between us. When she'd done it again, when she'd pulled me head, feet and all into her look, she'd turn away, and the shadows would flesh out again, and I'd have to ask the girls to repeat themselves. The cackle. Always the cackle, up the stairs, down to the cloakrooms. Her Tabitha cat.

Someone said that Catherine of Braganza had a rogue freckle. I've never seen it mentioned, certainly not portrayed, though the later Stuarts were my specialism. A different proposition, though, Catherine. Decorous, loyal to a king who didn't deserve it. Human.

3.

The outings were meant to sustain a sense of purpose once the GCSEs were over. They were carefully arranged, though the care did not extend to the choice of teachers to go on them. Short straws were the order of the day. When she heard which outing had chosen her, Elizabeth Ferguson pinned an index-card above her desk in the History Room: *SheerGlobe Park, Mon 2nd—no Phyll W!* Hopeful on Elizabeth's behalf, a colleague added a smiley face, but the smile said 'you'll be lucky.' Elizabeth tried to erase the face: it wouldn't budge.

Fog, she was known as: had been since her first term there. She knew her stuff—too thoroughly, which was perhaps why she'd earned the nickname. The need to strip her subject down for the lower years, to embroider precisely for those doing public exams, was one she could meet only fitfully. She never left pupils in the dark

23

but rather in a greyish dusk, which only a couple more well-chosen remarks would have cleared. A curious knowledge-lag settled about her methods. She'd arrive at the latest lesson to find a class who, by dint of extra reading or the interrogation of other staff on the qt, had only just understood the last one. She tried to be more unthinkingly pragmatic, but in her heart she taught for those who loved her subject. Like a music-hall trooper, she would happily play to an audience of three, two, one, while the rest were faces on the air.

Two years earlier, in her new GCSE group, one face had distinguished itself. It had a nose for incapacity; it knew how to pace effects. It announced itself sweetly: 'It's Phyll, miss. I do prefer Phyll.' Phyll didn't say much in the first term—even seemed to enjoy the Great Exhibition, the Indian Mutiny. But then she got her eye in. Bolshiness waxed and waned; salvos came hard, softened almost to gentle teasing, then came hard again. By the time Fog dragged them all into the Belle Époque, shortly before the final exams, the mood in the classroom belied the splendours of that age. In the midst of it all sat Phyll, dark goddess, loved by her familiars, loathed or feared by the rest, looking on her creation like an Ozymandias who hadn't lost out to sand.

Round the middle of Victoria's reign, Phyll opened up another front. If Fog was dealing with a crowd at the Staffroom door, if she was detaining a couple of girls over the Phoenicians or which was wattle and which daub, she'd sense ectoplasm thickening just out of sight—feel her concentration waning, her gaze itching to go elsewhere. Helpless, she'd let it. Then the presence was gone, triumphant, feet drumming.

This wasn't a new plan but a culmination. Before coming into Fog's orbit, Phyll had been weighing her up. When she was in the Upper Fourth, she'd sometimes wait for friends who were in Fog's lessons, giggling with them when they came out, casting a backward glance at her mark. One coffee break, a colleague sought Fog out in the Staffroom: 'Message, Elizabeth—that Dempsey girl at the door in tears, apparently.' There was no-one. Fog peered down Long Hallway. The edges of a claret jumper, a grey skirt, were just visible behind a far pillar. 'Sara Dempsey?' called Fog. The clothing seemed to shrink into the wall.

Fog sought help. Her Head of Department talked herself into and out of action: 'So I could have a word,' she concluded, 'but it wouldn't be the same as from you. Mightn't that'—she squeezed out a faux-pained smile—'make it worse?' Phyll's housemistress raised the drawbridge: 'I've had worse than her. Is she a pain? Yes. But we get her back into line.' 'So you're the useless one?' said the eyes of Phyll's mother.

4.

Fog got the full gen on *SheerGlobe Park* a week before the Upper Fifth outing, devoting a free lesson to its study. It was a chunk of bizarrerie between Birmingham and the Warwickshire countryside, an amusement park threaded about a scale replica of the world. It seemed to her that its constructors had started with one set of plans, picked up another by mistake and just gone on building. As she read, Phyll slid into her mind, obliging her to read bits again, to turn the maps this way and that. Phyll did the bare-wrist routine, a staple of the lateness she so lovingly shaped. In she'd come, choosing just that moment when any teacher might start to hope she was sick:

'I'm sorry, Fog...er, Miss Ferguson. My watch stopped.'

Protruding from a ruinous sleeve, the unadorned wrist would draw sniggers from cronies, 'do-something-Miss' looks from the rest. The performance offended Fog aesthetically no less than on a point of behaviour. Croakily executed, marked by that clunky pause after 'Fog,' it was as close as the girl got to invention. *SheerGlobe* ™ *prides itself on the detail with which the Americas are made yours to explore*, Fog read for the third time, only to find a familiar conversation breaking in, her actual words alternating with the responses she'd so often read behind Phyll's eyes:

'We've had the stopped-watch business before, Phyll.'

'Yes, and you'll have it again. Five minutes wasted.'

'Well, go and sit down.'

'You won't get that time back. Some thicko here won't understand something now, and they'll fail their exam.'

'Don't just stand there, Phyll. We're not waiting for nightfall.'

'Just as well, eh, Fog? Nothing doing for you then. No bloke with his thing out.'

'Can't you ask someone the time?'

'Can't you disappear up your arse?'

But then Phyll disappeared, and Fog found herself being lectured by the *SheerGlobe* booklet. A woman's voice, somehow restrained and ebullient, was urging delights upon her:

Amble down Highway 1, Maine to Florida, Fort Kent to Key West. Lose yourself in the autumnal shades of New England, the jazziness of Atlantic City, the kaleidoscopic Carolinas, the Florida swelter. Swing west to Galveston across our splendid Gulf Arc-way. The other Americas await—yours for the taking. Beauty awaits! Triumph awaits!

Fog tried re-reading those last exclamations. They weren't there, but they were in the room, shimmery assertions from the voice that was a scream inside a murmur. Fog pressed the back of the booklet, wondering if there was a tiny speaker, like in those awful birthday cards. She couldn't feel anything. What beauty? What triumph? Maybe she'd read them elsewhere in the thing. Maybe she was just hearing things, dog-tired.

A knock at the door made her stomach ice up. Didn't that bloody girl have other lessons? Like the bare-wrist nonsense, this other routine, empty-landing-with-figure-in-cranny, had worn beyond thin. But it was Abigail Swann, a plodder in her Lower Sixth group.

'Abi!'

The blast of relief nearly floored Abigail: 'I can come back, Miss,' she said, already retreating.

Geoff Youghall did nothing for me. Oh, he was entertaining, especially before our main teaching practice. Geoff in that seminar room, jigging round us, preaching avoidance—of staff-room hassle, basic errors, teaching itself if possible. *Now, those of you on practice at any place built on the vertical. Use the stairs but get them to use the lifts. Lifts can*

27

be made to get stuck. And book out dvds, a golden cache of them, days, weeks, aeons in advance. Any topic.

Jolly Geoff. But he never said a thing about what happens if you're thrown into that final room. If you're swept through all the others, past *inattentive, miserable, shy, clownish, tetchy* and find yourself there, in the dark, with that thing hunkered down, cuffing the foul air, making to spring. A feaster on faint souls. The thing it is, like rain is wet and airports are dreadful. An eternal evil.

SheerGlobe Park, Mon 2nd—no Phyll W! The Friday before the outing, Fog unpinned the card above her desk and went to see the Headmistress. Both women were in unquiet territory: Fog found it difficult to talk to the Head; the Head saw the need for a decision in the offing, an eventuality from which, over time, she'd shielded herself with a ring of deputies: 'We're talking entitlement, Elizabeth. Welford's as much as any other girl's.' Fog said nothing; in her pocket, the card was passionately squished. The Head watched her: not the happiest appointment, she reflected. Poor girl would do better hidden in an archive. Frowning, she calculated: 'I'm assuming there'll be more than one coach on Monday?'

'I should think so, Headmistress.'

'Well…leave with, and'—momentarily, the Head felt a touch giddy—'I'll certainly…I'll look into…'

Hurrying back to the History Room, Fog passed a couple of Phyll's cronies:

'…her cousin's a comp-oik and he said their top year's going.'

'What, this Monday as well?'

28

'Pass.'

'Well, find out, numpty. She'll want to know.'

5.

Autumn in midsummer. Mists low about the coach-park. A mass of girls being barked at. Behind them, a triumphal arch: *SheerGlobe*™ *You Are Here! You Are Everywhere!* Alongside it, a colossal map, bridges like harpoons connecting land to land.

'Everyone back at six. This spot. And remember, you are emissaries—I heard that, Lily Pedmore—yes, and I'll arrange for more than your boobs to freeze off. You are emissaries of Belvoir.'

There was a trilling at the edge of the group: 'It's them,' said someone. 'That coach over there.'

'Quiet!'

In front of their coaches, Fog and her colleagues watched Mrs Dellow wind up to the dismissal. Mrs Cotterill, Fog's companion on coach one, studied the *SheerGlobe* arch and shook her head:

'Preposterous. Still, I'll try Andalusia. I was set for the real thing last year—do some proper painting. But James had his bad fall.'

'I may walk barefoot to Palestine.' Fog and Mrs Cotterill turned to the hatcher of this plan. Mr Vallins, Mrs Dellow's sidekick on coach two, irritated Fog. Awkward, oily, he should have been the prime target for Phyll and her lieutenants. Instead, he awoke their motherliness, though this did not stop them thinking him a touch pervy and claiming that he always asked each new female teacher, single or not, for a date. He

29

was full of literary quotes, though he couldn't remember where most came from. Mercifully for the state of English teaching, he was leaving Belvoir at the end of the week, not for another post.

Mrs Cotterill gave him an unsunny smile: 'Whatever takes your fancy, dear.'

'Sorry, Phyllis?' Mrs Dellow cupped an ear theatrically. 'Yes, you *will* see the four of us around. Right, you've got your tickets and lunches. Now get in there!'

Fog studied the ground. She'd been spared for the journey up, but that meant the girl would be goaded by lost time. Surely there was somewhere in the world she could hide? Greenland…too exposed. Africa…perilous landscapes: she saw herself in a ravine, her ankle twisted, Phyll easing herself leisurely down the side—

'Casablanca?' Mrs Cotterill was saying to her. 'There's the *Humph and Ingrid* tea-shop, God help us. Meet you there at four?'

Fog nodded as Mrs Dellow strode up: 'Cheeky madam,' she muttered. 'I tell you, if Welford does come back in the Sixth, she can forget Physics.' She stared hard at Fog. *You're a poor thing,* said the stare. *We've got to beat her kind together.* 'Seems our local comp are here, too,' she added, 'so see you all on patrol. We don't want any nonsense. Right, I'm off to Saxony.'

'I was just saying to Elizabeth…' Mrs Cotterill turned, but Fog wasn't there.

Beyond the pines, the first carousel of the day was grinding. Fog looked up at the greenery all round her. Phyll wouldn't come near Norway. A boring place for boring people, she'd think it. But that was precisely why she might: 'This lesson's teeee-jious, Miss,' echoed in Fog's head. A commotion made her turn, braced to see those shoulders crushing nature as the girl and her cronies broke through. It was only a bird. Fog shivered: she could have gone to Andalusia with Mrs Cotterill— but, sweet though she was, her monologues, in which painters past and present were dreamily confused, would have been hard going for a whole day. Still, she couldn't stay here. Dammit, why shouldn't she see the world? Bad enough that the girl owned Belvoir without…

Her thoughts failed. Here was the booklet voice again, the woman behind the Americas blurb. Louder and louder she grew, until Fog wondered whether she'd leaned against a concealed audio feature: *Make your way. The Atlantic is a mere puddle. Stray into New England. Why wouldn't you? What is there here of beauty?* Fog gripped a branch for support. *Why wouldn't you?* the voice blasted now. *What is there here of triumph?*

Like someone learning to walk again, Fog embarked on the North Sea Pedway, cutting under Iceland, seeing the Faroes flow past her like skimming-stones. Soon the Pedway meshed with Atlantic Grove, tree-lined, lapped with blue, which brought her in south of Newfoundland, heading for Cape Cod. The sluggish mist lay low on Nantucket Island, but then it raised an edge, revealing a familiar stockiness, squared shoulders, the girl staring far down the seaboard. *Triumph,* wheedled the voice again. 'Whose triumph?' cried Fog. 'Who are you?'—at which Phyll turned, recognising the figure on the Atlantic. 'She's done it,' thought Fog, not knowing whether she meant the voice or Phyll. 'I'm bonkers.'

At that moment, Phyll was ambushed by two figures flying up from the south. Fog recognised them as the cronies she'd passed the previous Friday. The ensuing chat was brief and hysterical, ending with all three regarding Fog, who whispered 'That's it—b&b, Nether Stowey, smiles for my guests, guide-books in the sitting-room.' For a moment the girls were irresolute, but then Phyll shook her appalling hair, gestured 'She'll keep' and shot off ahead into New Jersey.

Follow, said the voice. Making landfall at New Haven, Fog wondered if some clip-on speaker had snagged about her clothes. She patted herself exhaustively: nothing. Still, she was calmer now. Better to be behind that trio, in control of distances. The accidental hunter. *Seek and hide,* the voice commanded. This, she reckoned, was as safe as she'd be. Beyond New Haven, Highway 1 opened at her feet. She set off, deciding that she was probably passing a string of artfully hidden tannoys.

The mist was lifting to a clear day. Sound carried. There still weren't many normal people about, thought Fog. Probably enough of them equated July with school excursions and postponed. From the distance came squeals: Belvoirians, no doubt, clustered in a pocket Manhattan or running for the Pacific Palisades. Something like a water-chute exploded. She hardly noticed Maryland, and Virginia only forced itself on her attention because the voice urged her to hurry out of Richmond. 'This is as fast as I go,' said Fog aloud. 'I don't want to clatter into them.' Then she heard.

Dear God, it was unmistakeable. It split the air

between lessons, at Christmas dinners. It came mockingly when prizes were dished out, when the new head girl was announced. A yowl, it was, exultant, claiming all as its own. She'd let rip with one once when Fog asked them to name Victoria's last prime minister. Chilled the bones, it did. Dissolved them.

But it was welcome now, repeating away, creating a map on the summer air. Fog could measure her distance from it as it drew her through the Carolinas and Florida to the coral-backed Keys. Again it came, out of the south. She took the Gulf Arc-way to Galveston, as the booklet voice had insisted in the quiet of the History Room. *Mexico, Honduras, Colombia,* intoned the voice now. *Dally at Barranquilla. Prepare, oh, prepare.*

'Steady on,' said Fog, a little breathless now. 'I can't forget Casablanca. Mrs Cotterill, four o'clock.'

Prepare! shrilled the voice. Chastened, Fog headed for the Panama Canal.

To the west of the Canal Zone was a prettified customs-house: hanging baskets, whitewashed veranda, huge windows. Deserted. Still, Fog fished in her bag: the main ticket doubled as a Panama Pass, and an attendant was bound to spring up. She heard voices far to the south, all strident, some deep, then the yowl again—but different now. There were squeals, closer, closer. Fog slid round the side of the customs-house, just in time to see Phyll's cronies pelting out of Colombia towards the Zone bridge, weeping, one holding her sides. The Zone attendant pursued them: 'Keep to the paths!' he panted. 'And where's the lippy one?' Reaching the bridge, he glanced through the customs-house windows: 'With you in a minute, miss,' he cried. The girls might have looked, too, but Fog ducked.

Fog dallied at Barranquilla. The yowls could have been arrows at her feet, so surely did they guide her. They came like keening now, throbbing between defiance and something else. She had no need to strain for the booklet voice: it was inside her. When she moved on, she fancied that *SheerGlobe* had become the real thing and she was striding gigantically through the patchwork of Old World findings and keepings. Occasionally she closed her eyes, letting Phyll's yowls pull her through Venezuela and Guiana like a wind of strange comfort. At the mouths of the Amazon, a last yowl yanked her inland, off the path: *Manaus Hinterlands* said a sign, loosing her into a tunnel of thick leaves. She nearly blundered straight into the clearing, into the circling group, but she braked and the leaves held her fast.

The leader was a girl. She leaned, taking her weight on the front foot like a ballerina. Her move seemed like one of a sequence, as did the stretch of her hand, the hard flick:

'Say again?'

Facing her, cheeks crimson, that lone freckle looking darker, uglier, Phyll worked her mouth. The group, boys and girls, moved a step closer. The girl rocked back, giving the circle a look of parental exasperation. Again she leaned, demanded. Fog thought her beautiful. She seemed like an angel sent down to the mud of the earth on a vital dirty errand. Even the next flick of her hand spoke of immortal blessing.

Phyll answered: a shriek, high and scrawny, blowing holes in the air, resolving itself as 'Plebby, plebby, slum-scum, plebby.' The girl tightened, baring fox-teeth, swinging her hands in slow motion at Phyll's head. The circle closed.

I swallowed hard. She had to say it. Just couldn't help herself. The circle—were they all dancers? Goodness, it was so neatly done—a foot round the ankle, a shove, arms and hands right in there like they were dragging hay from a rick. The feet, feet, feet. And in the end, that lardy body wrapped about the leader's calf like a stuck earwig. No sound. All her yowls gone like sewer-gas. Then, dammit, crying girls thumping in from somewhere, an official voice yelling 'I've got better things…', and bloody Mrs Dellow with her 'Can't you girls…what kind of example?' Wrecking the beauty.

But the dancers got out. Pairs of soles rocketing through the green. I waited long enough to see Dellow kneel, hear her own yowl. Then I inched away, got my shoes off, ran—Canal Zone deserted—ran—Mexico silent. And there he was at Texas, the pathetic Vallins, mooning about. I was too slow onto the Gulf Arc-way: 'Aha Elizabeth,' says he, doffing a pretend hat, probably floppy, possibly mauve. 'Went the day well?' That look. I can see why the girls stick their fingers in their mouths.

6.

Fog answered the questions precisely. Yes, she saw the girls running back across the Panama Canal. No, she didn't hail them. Sorry? Just high spirits, presumably: exams over, off the leash. Yes, they might well have seen her. To be honest, she was rather more concerned about finding her ticket, which (here she proudly quoted the booklet verbatim) doubles as a pass for the Panama Canal, the Pyramids, the Vatican and the coves of Tasmania.

The man nodded. At his side, the WPC smiled. Fog craved dismissal. If this was *SheerGlobe's* idea of a manager's office, something was greatly skewiff. Poky, it was, dust-filled. Was that a cigar she could smell?

'They gave the attendant a run for his money,' said the man.

'Yes…poor chap.'

'Doing his duty.' The man looked at her levelly.

'Well I suppose—'

'And where did you go after that?'

'Oh…down south, you know.'

'And you didn't see anything?'

'To be honest'—Fog wavered, then plunged—'I rather lost my way. Hot lands aren't really my thing. When I got my bearings, I ran back.'

'Ran?'

Ran! pounced the voice. Fog swallowed: 'In a manner of speaking.'

Outside, an engine started up, then another.

'Your coaches.' The man sniffed. 'Someone's trying to tell us something.' The WPC whispered and made to rise.

'No, no, it's fine, Miss Ferguson's our last,' he said. 'I think we've pretty well…' He tapped her note-book: 'We have home address and number?'

The WPC flipped a page and read them out for Fog's confirmation. Fog and the man rose:

'Well, if we don't meet again—' He extended a hand.

Fog tried a sparkle: 'I shan't skip the country.'

The man cocked his head: 'But you did. All day. So to speak.'

Fog hurried for the coach. All she wanted was to flop down by Mrs Cotterill, let her noodle on about the *Humph and Ingrid* Café in Casablanca ('Don't worry that you clean forgot,' she imagined her saying, 'in the circs. Dreadful place. And, my God, the price of the lattes') and spend the journey staring at the start of life, the glorious colour of the days to come. Odd, that man was. *If we don't meet again.* Why would they? He practically called her tail-end Charlie.

As she climbed into her coach, she invited the *SheerGlobe* voice to speak her exultation. There was a crackle, then nothing.

7.

Sweet of the Head to get me on the quiet like that—last day, so much going on. So many headaches for her. I saw her yesterday with the Bursar, staring at chaos. What to do after Monday's events? How to ensure all the girls returned in September? Well, he could charm the pips from an orange. She can lean on him.

'Elizabeth,' she murmured, 'I've told the other staff from'—she jiggled her hand to fill in the venue and calamity—'that they don't have to come to Grand Commem this afternoon. So you just—'

Then her secretary came up: 'Telephone. Lydia

Hallwood's parents—again. Say they'll send her back next term if there's a rebate.' Poor dear Head—she aged twenty years as she turned away.

She'd go up to Phyll's boarding-house, station herself discreetly. Apparently the mum and dad were coming to pack up. An event to savour. Well, she was excused the nonsense of Grand Commem, and her parents weren't expecting her till evening. Oh, she knew what most would say about her intent. What of it? You didn't need a cathedral for commemoration. Doubtless the voice would join her, freed from the booklet, the hidden wires of that terrible place, and be her co-celebrant. She pictured the hatchback of some gas-guzzler, Mr Phyll heaving stuff in any-old-how, Mrs checking her hair in the paintwork, the housemistress all clucks.

At lunchtime, breezing up the main stairs, she saw her Head of Department, wished her a happy summer and waited for the same.

'Souvenir for you,' said her head, gesturing up to the History Room.

'From—?' began Fog, but the woman just shrugged and sailed on down.

Fog banged open the History Room door. On her desk lay a sheet of paper folded round a leaf of Brazil.

Come, Holy Ghost

For Gill Pardoe, Monday was a wide, plunging path. You looked at it from above and slightly to the left. High hedges ran alongside it. Where it ended wasn't clear: briars, possibly. Wednesday was a gently arching bridge you looked at from some way off. You could be a wanderer at rest on a river stone, hailing travellers as they straggled across. Friday was another plunge. This time, though, it ended in a den of soft grasses. You could lie there, head cushioned, looking up. Between you and the sky there were faces, leaning over the den's rim. They weren't unfriendly and their mouths worked away, but you couldn't hear what they said. They were still stuck somewhere in the humdrum days you'd shaken off—in a Tuesday afternoon, say, at around twenty to three.

Since childhood, Gill Pardoe had seen the invisible. Nothing had taught her how. There had been no magic revelation tricked out with lights and echoes: it was just there. Like an assiduous dresser, she'd spent her life clothing abstractions in their proper fit and style. Overheard arguments were a mass of raised hands with spikes coming out of the wrists. Blandishments were a waiter with little tureens of melted chocolate balanced up his arms. But the waiter was dopey, or drunk. The tureens slopped this way and that. Drip by drip, his arms bled dark brown. Everything was a mess.

School was an inevitable problem. After all, what safe home could there be for her visions among the satchels and vaulting horses, the mix of scant praise and bleak

39

warning that was morning assembly? Gill turned a look of vacancy on her schooldays. Clips round the ear were not unknown, nor was adult despair at her perennial dreaming. When she was thirteen, her class was the first to get a movable blackboard. Teachers would haul it out at an angle or shove it flat against the wall, as enthusiasm or anger dictated. Gill liked it best at an angle. From her desk, she gazed at the gap between board and wall. She saw a house. At its front door, a woman who wasn't her mother hailed her with surpassing affection. Beside the woman, a man used words she'd never heard from her father: questions about how her day had been, advice on how to treat a world that was just a rubbish-tip of facts.

'Tea's on the table,' the woman once said. 'Your favourite.' Obediently, she had gone to tea—only to be bundled back to her desk before tasting a mouthful. The next day, her real mother and father sat either side of her in that same classroom. Before them, her form teacher described the future that awaited a girl who seemed determined to be absent from her own life. For days after, she lived with her parents' displeasure. A thick, black fur, it was, smelling of open drains.

Yet the future brought marriage, children, a string of tolerable jobs. Gill found that she could perform as required. Somehow she accepted that life was a double-image, though the images were chalk and cheese. Saying 'I do' at the altar, getting up at two am at the summons of infant cries, remembering to put her work-coat on this peg, not that one—these were just passing shadows. She served them without murmur. But then her own realities would gently insist. She would walk through

40

some open space and feel it pitch and lunge, a mother-ship riding the atmosphere of a new planet like a feather on a breeze. Listening to the chat of other mothers at the school gates, she would see unknown animals with coloured voices: harsh orange, yellowy-white. Sometimes a voice was light blue, the colour of comfort. That was rare.

She hadn't been expecting trouble from the Holy Ghost. She wasn't expecting it to figure in her life at all. Faith hadn't, not really. Her parents' many edicts had been purely secular. Her children were baptised, but that was thanks to a doting father who wouldn't leave anything to chance. Her main involvement there was ensuring that, in his transport of pride, he didn't bump their heads on sacred stone. She couldn't remember the Holy Ghost being mentioned then—or at her wedding. References to it might have come and gone at her schools: after all, they were C of E. But that would have been part of the adult burble that chafed at her visions like grit in a comfy shoe. And wasn't it 'Holy Spirit' anyway? Didn't Catholics say 'Holy Ghost'?

Thinking this, Gill remembered Amy Bracewell. When she was nine, she and Amy had been pen-pals. Gill couldn't recall what they had in common. There must have been enough, though, to warrant that visit to Amy's house in Harrogate. And yes…yes, the Holy Ghost had stepped in there. Amy's parents were Catholic: very devout. There'd been evening prayers; special guest or not, Gill had been obliged to join in. She and Amy (and possibly a sibling or two) had knelt down at chairs and sofas in the lounge. The more Gill thought

41

about it, the clearer the memory became. Yes, she was directed to an armchair with an old fug of human smells in its cushion. Turning her head to avoid them, she'd rested an ear against the cloth. So it was that she'd heard all the praying as a mass of vibrations, in which 'The Holy Ghost' had resonated with particular depth.

But that was nearly fifty years ago. It hardly counted as some kind of sign, did it? She'd thought the whole prayer business peculiar, but no worse than most of the world's carry-on. The experience hadn't left her with any urge to wrap the Holy Ghost in a vision—certainly not the urge that grew in her now.

She tried telling herself that it was all about unfairness. And bad art. Unfairness because, from what she knew, the Holy Ghost was forced to tag along after the Father and the Son. It was treated like a pudgy kid next door: someone given bit parts in the important games of others. As for the bad art, that certainly appeared to be what turned Gill Pardoe—fifty-something wife and mother, rejecter of a ticky-tacky world—into a woman possessed. For weren't ghosts the ultimate abstraction? And among them, didn't a Holy Ghost deserve all the care that imagination could lavish? You wouldn't think so, she told herself as she started on her rounds. A hunch led her to an illustrated Bible in some far shadow of the loft. She moved silently along aisles of neglected churches, squinting at tableaux in prayer-books. Saturdays found her in Christian bookshops, one step ahead of baffled assistants. Finally, she bought *A Young Celebrant's Catechism*, all big print and plenty of pictures. Back home, she laid it out on the kitchen table alongside the illustrated Bible, and stared from one to the other. They were typical of everything she'd seen. She couldn't believe that the Holy Ghost could be so ill-served. All of those ignorantly-applied primary colours, those thick black lines. Floppy wings, appalling smears of light. She could do better. Someone had to.

Only she couldn't. When she closed her eyes, all she saw was a tunnel of November mist. There was something at the very end of it: some form wavering darkly. Despite her efforts, it never came closer. She grew afraid. What was really impelling her to do this? And was it a vision too far for her powers? She tried everywhere—in the quiet of the bathroom, amid crowds who came at her as though she were a ghost herself. Still the form lurked at the end of the tunnel, defiant in its vagueness. She grew haggard, listless at home, inattentive at work.

New and strange, the notion that came to her then. None of her previous visions had ever required practical preparation: it was superfluous. But perhaps not now. However alien it felt, she needed advice. Then, perhaps, the tunnel of mist might furl away and the Holy Ghost—her Ghost—might come to her, clad as he should be.

Father Deeley kept calling her Mrs Parker, then apologizing, then saying it again. But he was flustered. Turning from the lectern in his empty church, he'd found Gill hanging over the altar rail, looking like a boat passenger who bitterly regrets their voyage. He offered her tea, the comfort of the church's social centre. She declined both. Her questions were urgent, sharply-voiced. They didn't stop while he guided her to a front pew. Their effect was to make him realize, for the first time in his vocation, that he didn't like the pent-up smells that collided in a church. This disconcerted him even more.

'Oh, no,' said Father Deeley. 'I wouldn't call the Holy Ghost hard done by, Mrs Parker—Pardoe.' He said that the Holy Ghost was often referred to first, or alone. It had its own complement of hymns: 'Come, Holy Ghost' was one of the best known. He found himself singing it, only stopping when he saw the look on Gill's face. You could argue, he pressed on, that saying 'and Holy Ghost' gave it a status that neither the Father nor the Son could claim. That simple word 'and' fixed its divinity in people's minds. It confirmed the Holy Ghost as the Almighty's candle, illuminating Father and Son. How could they burn bright if it were not in glorious attendance?

Gill surprised him—surprised herself—with a smile. He hoped that it meant understanding, not confused indulgence. To be on the safe side, he was just about to launch into the New Testament when a noise made them both turn. At the back of the church, one of the deacons was shuffling and beckoning.

'Would you excuse me?' whispered Father Deeley. Creaking up the aisle, he joined the deacon, who gestured again. They went across to the social centre. On her own, Gill continued to smile. The priest's words drifted through her mind like eddying leaves. *Illuminating.*

44

Bright. At last she looked about her as an artist might survey a studio, satisfied that all was to hand—as indeed it was. No, she'd never required preparation before. Perhaps, because of it, all the visions to come would be immense, spellbinding.

Father Deeley was gone a goodly while. Whatever his business with the deacon, it made him forget about Gill. He might not have returned, had the deacon not glanced out at the church and asked if the timer for the main lights was still playing up. Father Deeley looked. The church windows were ablaze. They hurried over, dragging open the door, to be met by pulsations of light, clouds of smoke whose hugeness suggested giant rams with heads down. Every candle, it seemed, had been lit. Even in the murk, it was obvious that books and hangings were on fire. Father Deeley mimed a phone call and the deacon vanished. Alone, the bewildered priest stumbled further into the church, just able to make Gill out amid the horns of smoke. She seemed to be kneeling, her head slumped against the pew seat. In the confusion of smoke and flame, she looked scarcely bigger than a girl.

Gill's head was turned sideways. The smoke was pricking her eyes, scratching under her clothes. But the wood of the pew was a patch of cool against her cheek. For a little longer she breathed freely, untroubled by any smells ingrained in the pew—any ghostly intimations of mortal worship. Something began to burn about her haunches, then traced a mortifying hand along her spine. In her mind, the November mist cleared, revealing the form that had teased her for so long. It turned—almost casually, like someone struck by an afterthought. No longer in thrall to the meanness of page or tapestry, it moved, approached. Flourished.

First published in *Under The Radar—Nine Arches Press—issue 12, December 2013*

Misshapes From Cadbury's

1.

There's just the one light, shadeless, on a little table that looks like it began life as a cotton spool. The bulb casts an aspiring glow. Beside the table, blankets froth onto a chair which, at some point, must have been easy. Now it just looks tired of human weight.

The chair starts to disappear—the seat, the worn flowers across the back. She lowers herself with the careful management of two sticks, whose handles fall against her shoulders when she's done. Her rhythmic breathing seems vital to the manoeuvres: *vof vof vof,* ending with a blissful *hawwff* when, fully berthed, she looks up. I wonder if I'm meant to respond with a *hawwff* of my own, as a compliment on her skill or vicarious enjoyment of her transition from peril to repose.

'Oh? Oh?' she says now, turning to either stick. She sounds maternal. The sticks could be a couple of kids, pushing their luck past bed-time. More *vof-vofs*, her cheeks fluttering against her breath. Even in proper light they would look yellow. I take a guess, step forward, lift the sticks away. Now she's ready for words: 'Just there,' she says. Then, as I stow them by the spool of a table, 'It's been a day.' A month before I would have frowned. England's English: it's been a twisty business, watching how native words can play truant from guides and grammar-books. A word would turn its underside to me, leave me clueless.

My Uncle Padmore, nimblest filing-clerk in Grenada,

had tried to brief me. He'd lived here for a while before England went decimal. 'Incredible,' he said. 'In some shop, your counter-guy adding up the bill. "Right," he says, "one-and-one and one-and-one is two-and-two." What was that? Magician talk? Good job you going now. Now, the money means what it says.'

It's been a day. A month ago the words would have grazed me like low furniture. Yes, it has, I would have thought. We've had the morning and the noon, and now the kitchens of the land are clattering with the fact of tea. And the sticks I've stowed away have been an old lady's added legs. Now they're dull strips of wood; soon they'll be legs again. But then I began to watch for words at their clowning. A milestone was when someone said, 'Well, there's a thing,' and I didn't look around.

'Yes,' I say now, looking down at the small figure *vof-voffing* again. 'Yes, it has been a day.' And she knows that I know.

2.

I called out three times. Each time the postman accelerated a little more into the fog. I'd just come downstairs when the letterbox made its woodpecker sound and a splash of post, mostly for the previous occupant, lay about the floor. On the back of one piece, a cheery invitation to a special event for discounted flak-jackets, there was a scribble: *Parcel*, it said, *out front.*

David Bedworth. That was the previous occupant. For a spell, when I'd first moved in, it had been David and June Bedworth, but then she'd disappeared from the front of the envelopes. Perhaps there'd been an almighty row; perhaps he was spending his nights at other kinds of event. Either way, the post had never featured Amy Fothergill. But there she was, inscribed on a soft, bulky parcel which fell against my feet as I opened the door. I ran to the pavement. The postman was just emerging two doors down. I tried 'Excuse me,' 'I'm sorry' and 'This isn't mine,' but my words only pushed him into one of the alleys that criss-crossed the neighbourhood: time warps, perhaps, for public servants with a cold day and a dog-infested route before them.

In the kitchen, I dithered with the address on the parcel and a map of the town. That evening, I dithered again in the kitchen of the couple next door. 'It's somewhere near,' Thelma kept assuring me.

Harold glowered at the map. 'Bentley Cross way, I think,' he murmured. 'Proper warren, those streets.' Thelma beamed at me, ready, perhaps, with a description of warrens and their inhabitants. 'Gotcha!' Harold stabbed at the eastern reaches of the town. 'Mmm…goodish walk.'

'I wouldn't trouble, love,' said Thelma. 'Take it to the delivery office, I should.'

But in the brief time I'd had it, the parcel had made a new corner in my life. For the first time in this country, I'd been nominated as custodian. Accident had pulled aside the routine web of human action and said, 'See to this.'

'It's fine,' I said to Thelma. 'If I can't find it, I'll—'

'Here.' Harold inscribed a neat cross on Amy Fothergill's street. 'Take a flask,' he winked.

'Brandy,' elaborated Thelma, 'in case you get lost. It's

49

what they…'

The remainder of her twinkly explanation followed me to the door.

3.

Next day there was a by-election, and my workplace was in use for polling. The fog was back. I might have packed some brandy, only I had a bad memory of having it forced on me as a child by Restless Headey, a character back home in Harford Village, amid much joshing from my father, who was indebted to Headey in some way I never discovered. "Las, 'las,' said Headey as I pitched and spluttered: a strange word, but he was an English teacher, one of the fiercest in Grenada, with a special passion for John Webster, and he was forever pinching the man's language. At the time, he and my father had laughed mightily.

On the way home, though, I got a terrible dig in the back: 'You should've drunk it down,' hissed my father. He would have, and then some.

As it was, I packed a bottle of water—I could imagine my father's snorting at that, then Headey's, even louder—stuffed the parcel into my rucksack and set off. As I walked, map in hand, the streets unfolded before me as nowhere ever had, not Harford Village, not St George's, not Grenada itself. It was as though the town had been aching to lay down its tangle of geography, and my mission was obliging it. Hedges and walls peeled away, alleys curved neatly into other alleys. In the fog-dulled air, police sirens sounded like the whistling we used to set up as kids at Fancy Min, self-styled toast of

50

Harford, when she was off on yet another doomed date. And suddenly, there I was, down an alley you could hardly turn in, looking from the parcel to the blistering cream door, checking the number on both, frowning at the card in the window, an inventory of business callers whom the occupant wished to repel. But I, postman for a day, wasn't among the despised.

I knocked for a longish while. At last a form appeared behind the door's patterned glass, its head perhaps level with my chest. I heard the word 'who?', then something I didn't catch, then 'who?' again. A face appeared above the baleful card at the window, eyes wide, cheeks wobbling like the gills of a harried fish. I imagined a cry, her hand on the phone, a posse of neighbours. Smiling foolishly, I held the parcel against the window, my finger pointing to the address like a 'You Are Here' symbol on the map that had served me so faithfully. Moments later, her papery face was sizing me up behind a door-chain. Again her eyes took in the parcel, and I'd just started on my prepared explanation about how her name came to be in my keeping when I saw them fill with tears. There was some clattering, the wobble of a stick, and then the chain swung free. I found myself in a room which, in its owner's sprightlier days, had probably been much loved.

Assuming that I was a true courier, Miss or Mrs Fothergill seemed ready to repose a degree of trust in me which, I uncomfortably realised, I was yet to earn. Still, having gone through a battery of checks to get to this country, this living room, I expected a demand for identification. None came. Instead, swaying on her sticks, blinking more tears away, she muttered: 'Could you open it, love?'

'Me? Lady, it's your post. As for me, I'm…who I am is…'

But she nodded away my babble, mouthing something which became words as I obediently slid my fingers about the parcel-seams: 'Ah, she's gone…she's gone.' The contents lay revealed in my hands: an item of clothing and a sturdy box in a clear plastic bag, topped by a letter. She stared at them; then, like a waking child, at me:

'Are you from Birmingham?'

'No, I just—'

'Have you had to come all that way with this?'

'I live in the town—your parcel was—'

'Oh, love us, she's gone.'

Her words nearly knocked her over. Dropping the parcel, I caught her by the shoulders, walking her backwards, sticks and all, to safety and rest. I saw the chair, well-blanketed, with its spread of dull flowers; and the unshaded lamp, doing its best against the fog. As she sank down, her hand scrabbled around the little table, finally hooking her glasses. Then, parcel on lap, she dispatched me to a kitchen the size of a lift, where, after several false starts, I assembled cups of tea and the last of some Christmas shortbread.

I was in shock. I feared that she was, too, and that, when I returned, she'd snap out of it and *'Police! Burglars! Help!'* would beat round the walls as they often did in those Ealing comedies my Uncle Padmore adored. But no. I was quaveringly instructed where to set the tea and shortbread, urged to tuck into the latter. Again I tried introducing myself but she forestalled me, raising the letter from the parcel in a way that made me think of Sunday School and all I hadn't learnt there.

The parcel had come from Maureen Day—or rather, on her behalf, from a nursing home up in Birmingham. No: no, you do things on behalf of the living. The parcel's contents—a cardigan and some bath salts, recent gifts from Amy—were not belongings now, but effects. Death had come for Maureen and, with sober tidiness, had exchanged one word for the other.

'Worked in the Ministry, we did,' said Amy. 'Twenty-five years.'

I was unsure if we were on sacred or governmental ground, but then she spoke of ration books: '1954, we dished out the last. For sweets. Next half-day we had, we took off to Bournville, Maureen and me. Got two heaping bagfuls of misshapes to celebrate—right from Cadbury's. Battled our way through all the kids in creation. Had to jump off the train at Stourbridge coming back, barricade ourselves in the Ladies. Sick as a pair of hounds.' Pausing, she laid a hand on the cardigan. 'Twenty-five years. Pal of pals, she was. It was turn and turn about between us.' I'd heard Thelma next door use and lengthily explain that term; my smile at Amy was properly knowing. 'She was my bridesmaid, I was hers. We went up to Wolverhampton, to the Midland Educational. Got some fancy parchment, two sheets apiece.' She *vof-voffed* happily, but my understanding was downed again. Did bridesmaids throw parchment over here? 'Family trees,' she said then. 'So we could set them down—our mums and dads, in-laws, kids when they

53

came along, their kids. Folk are daft about that stuff now. Ancestry. Paying someone a fortune to tell them what they want to hear. Well, we thought, why not do our bit? Save some great-great-great grandchild a pile of money.'

I thought of Amy or Maureen worrying over a gap in the parchment, dragging a husband off to bed so a baby could be organised to fill it. A rude notion. But even now, so early in our acquaintance, I hoped that Amy might chuckle if I said it.

'Then it's 1974,' she continued, steering a bit of shortbread into her tea. 'Boundary changes. Hereford and Worcester shoved together. Twenty-five years and the Ministry show us the door. Her hubby gets a job with Birmingham Council—and she's gone.'

'But you still saw her.'

'Still wrote. As for seeing...' Silence. Suddenly there was something she wasn't minded to show. Did the husbands not get on? Was there some jealousy over the friendship? Or something done and never spoken of— some danger that the marks on the two sheets of parchment might blend where they shouldn't?

She changed tack. We listened, the fog and I. It was a patchwork afternoon: more jollity from the Ministry years, the names and foibles of the kids who came along, the deaths of other halves. But then glancing details of a particular holiday they all took together, followed by another, longer silence. Perhaps now she was inviting a question. I couldn't find one—didn't think I should. Instead I passed the wordless minutes by wondering how she'd recognised the parcel. Maybe the nursing home had re-used one she'd sent before. Maybe it was Maureen's writing, intended for a parcel of her own, to be filled with—what? Happy remembrances of a friendship that had retreated to stamps and envelopes? More misshapes from Cadbury's?

'Who are you?' For an instant, I was unsure whether I'd heard the words or was getting another lordly grilling from Restless Headey after the other kids had gone home. I told her, and where I was from. She cocked her head. This was it: her involuntary grieving was done and she'd come to her senses. I braced myself to be stick-prodded into the fog, to see a downward swirl of old paint as the door slammed. But, seeing off a fresh tear, she smiled:

'Dignified name, that. But Grenada…oh, lovey, you're a long way away.'

Stock still, I felt like a precious waxwork: *Study with Tea and Crumbs.* Right now, I didn't say, we both were. In their different ways, death and distance had cut us loose. When she spoke again, jiggling the letter, saying that Maureen's funeral was the following Tuesday, that she'd no-one to go with and wondered—would? could?—I said yes.

4.

It's been a day. In that tight kitchen, I turn the phrase over. No shortbread now, but circular biscuits showing goofy faces as they land on the plate. A day of sustaining kindness. My remembered good fortune in getting to ask the nicer of my managers for time off. The taxi-driver who chatted all the way to Birmingham, who was a kid when they lifted rationing on sweets and who, like Amy and Maureen, dived into the chocolate mountain that peace had tardily created. The minister who didn't know Maureen, who could have simply dispatched her with flyblown words but instead had enfolded her in that love which nearly everyone deserves at the end. Presumably she'd quizzed the staff at the nursing home—done it expertly, it seemed, to judge from the number of times Amy said 'That was just like Mo' as another bit of her friend's life was released into the near-empty chapel. Feeling Amy's dependent sag against my shoulder, I tried to assemble those bits, ending up with another Amy: another pair of sticks to stow away, another length of shortbread to angle against a cup. It would have been nice to hear them commemorating their misshapes. For a moment, I mourned Maureen intensely, *vof-voffing* in my own way.

But it's been a day of silence, too. In the taxi home, I'd remarked that it was a shame that none of Maureen's family were there. Lips parting, Amy stiffened. Me, too. Dear God, not another mere pile of effects, not right here beside me.

'Her kids live abroad?' asked the taxi-driver at last, mercifully judging that we couldn't sit there with nothing but road-noise.

'In a manner,' said Amy.

'Of speaking?' I tried. But she did no more of that till we pulled up. Luckily, the taxi-driver was big on cricket and I found myself hearing all the stats I'd grown up with: 'Grenada? Ooh, Junior Murray, mate. 202 against Australia, '92-'93. He could knock them about.'

'You gone to Plymouth for that tea?' Her chuckles

draw me back into the living room where, setting out the cups and biscuits, I think of the weekly letter home I'm due to write: an old-fashioned custom, forced on me by cousin Devon, computer-mad but apt to delete e-mails at random, including the ones I've laboured over for distribution among the family. How will this letter go? Mentioning a funeral, certainly dwelling on it, might make them fret about how I'd managed, so soon, to stumble into the shadows of remote lives. But I have to say something. So…yes, lead off with Cadbury's, the misshapes, which would allow my Uncle Padmore to be wise and enlightening (to my father's irritation). From there I could swerve back to the parcel, the narrow path, the two sticks, the…but now there's a hand on my arm, clear eyes holding mine.

'Maureen and I,' says Amy. 'The things they said about us…her kids, her husband…'

Quietly, I'm ordered to sit down; reminded of the twenty-five years' worth of larks at the Ministry. But the voice doesn't sound like Amy's. Looking above her head, I see a shadow on the wall, darting, bowing, nothing to do with the weak lamplight, with my own bulk as I settle in my chair. 'Friendship takes in all sorts, young man,' continues…who?

I listen. Another voice briefly intrudes: my own, without sound, as I find the salutation for my letter home:

Dear One and All: Just today, the living and the dead confided…

First published in *Under The Radar—Nine Arches Press—issue 7, January 2011*

Halfway Through Bilston With Josef Locke

A slab of kaleidoscopic stone propped against a strip of willow. That was how he looked in the near-distance, among the signs for pubs and butchers, the angle-parked cars, all the casual furniture of a West Clare street on a midweek evening. A hulk of a man, he leaned on his stick one-handed, his riotous shirt and sky-blue trousers defiant against the failing August light. At first, as I approached, I thought he was frozen. Or that he'd passed on and was set to weather eternity in a pose of benign reflection. When I got close, however, I saw that his bald head was gently nodding: in time, I guessed, to the music from the session in the pub behind him.

I was headed there myself. Minutes earlier, agitated, showering myself in silent curses, I'd run out of it. Having stood a round for my group of family and friends, endured the usual exclamations of theatrical shock at my willing separation from my money and watched as the drinks appeared one by one on the counter, I'd remembered that my wallet was back in the car. No doubt someone else would have paid. The cost to me, however, would have been more than financial. I'd imagined—no, all but heard—the hoots of scorn as, turning from the bar, I confessed my plight. Probably I'd made things worse by scarpering without a word. But it wasn't a moment to pause and meditate on action and consequence.

Now, breezing past the swirly shirt, the nodding head,

I caught the words, 'Lovely music. Lovely.' Something made me stop dead: not, contrary to the robust belief in some quarters, a reluctance to sponsor the consumption of two Guinnesses, a red wine, two whites, a double whiskey and a diet something-or-other-with-a-twist. 'Lovely,' the man repeated, nodding his head in time to his syllables, gripping his stick with both hands. 'I'd still be in there if I hadn't needed this breath of fresh.'

There was a warm joy in his voice. Surprise, too—as though, all his life, he'd been tracking precisely that music in that place, never thinking he'd find them. But something else battled his delight: something in his breath's dry crackle, in the shiver which suddenly rocked his bulk as though it were no more than a leaf for the blowing. Pain, I guessed.

'So glad we came,' he said now, drawing me deeper into his regard. We might have been chatting all day. 'First time over here, and it nearly didn't happen. Dr Crowhurst, he said my ticker wouldn't be best pleased— the travel, all the in-and-out from the car. I should have done it years ago, he says, if I was that set on it. For good, perhaps. "You've been too long round Wolverhampton, Mr Robbins," he says. "You've got Black Country lung." Well, I go along next time'—lifting a hand from the stick, he gave a damp snap of the fingers—'and he's only changed his tune. "On reflection," he says, "why not do it?" Worth all the National Insurance I ever paid, those six words.'

I pictured my group staring at the drinks on the bar and the drinks staring back. But I couldn't move off now without seeming ignorant. 'Well,' I imagined saying, 'good on Dr Crowhurst. Take care, then.' It sounded crass. Besides, Dr Crowhurst had now stepped aside for Mr Aynscuff.

'Best teacher ever, him,' he said. 'Got me in on the school plays—doing lighting, sound effects. The sparks and spots, he called them. And he got me onto this'—he tilted his head in the direction of the music. 'He used to help out at Wolverhampton Grand, weekends and holidays. Both Hippodromes, too, Birmingham and Dudley. He got to know them all—properly, mind—phone calls, Christmas cards. Ruby Murray, Edmund O'Hagan. Put Christy Moore up on his first trip to England. Josef Locke.'

At the last name, the music inside seemed to melt. Odd discords surfaced. A squeezebox sounded as though it was dropping its notes like beads all over the floor. Had my group given up on me, and were they now plying the musicians with my round—and many more—on the assurance that the escapee with the cash would be marched back in to foot the bill? Then I realized that, swaying on his stick, Mr Robbins was overlaying their current reel with Josef Locke. *Girls Were Made To Love and Kiss* issued from his lips in a wavery but committed baritone. After a few lines he stopped. 'Taught me that,' he said, face flushed with effort and happiness. 'Mr Locke.'

I was vaguely conscious of a figure at the pub door. It could have been a banished smoker. It could have been one of my group, perhaps drawing a finger across their throat, signalling the fate of drink defaulters. I took no notice.

60

'The last Christmas I was at school,' said Mr Robbins. 'Mr Aynscuff comes by the house. Do I want extra present money? He's helping backstage at Wolverhampton Grand and they need another pair of hands. Can't remember who was on. Tommy Trinder, maybe. Arthur Askey. Afterwards, "I'll give you a lift home," says Mr A. "Car's just round in Marchant Street. Be with you in a tick." I get round there—only car in sight's a Bentley. Bit of a step up from Mr A's Standard Ten. But that wasn't about, nor nothing else. The door was unlocked—well, you could do that in those days. So in I jump. Leather seats, radio. Palace on wheels. "What's he hired this for?" I wondered. Anyway, after a minute drumming my fingers, I couldn't resist—slid myself over to the wheel, started turning it—hard left, hard right, you know, like a kid thinks it's done. All of a sudden there's this voice at the back of my neck. Nearly sends me through the roof. "I'm having second and third thoughts about you as my cabbie." I look in the mirror'—his voice dropped reverently—'and it's only him! Mr Locke! "So, away to Birmingham, is it?" he says. "Will I serenade the night owls in the Bull Ring?"'

I stared hard at Mr Robbins. Now he was completely still. His look was almost boyish, as though the Wolverhampton memory had lifted the yoke of years from his back. I half expected him to throw away the stick and turn a cartwheel.

'Then Mr Aynscuff gets in, and I shove over again for Mr Locke's real driver. Both of them hooting away—kindly, though, like they were telling me it was OK to be confused and chuffed at the same time. Turned out Mr

61

Locke was playing Birmingham the next night. Came up to catch the show at the Grand. So there's me, passenger of honour, being chauffeured home—Willenhall, quite a way up the road. Home James! In a Bentley, mind you, with—' He broke off, as though the use of the famous name was a thing to be carefully rationed. 'Singing away, we were,' he continued. '*Moonlight and Roses, I'll See You In My Dreams, Shrimp Boats*, anything. Well, nearly anything. The driver starts on with *Heartbreak Hotel*. "Hey, not in this car," says Mr Locke. "Don't remind me of the competition." Like a drain, he was, laughing. He does a solo—*The Desert Song.*' He shook his head. 'Magic, that.'

'Then, halfway through Bilston, he asks me to sing one of his songs on my own. His, mind! Well, I knew them but I didn't—see what I mean? I listened to them, loved them, but I was a kid, you know? Head full of all sorts. I had scraps of them, but that was it. I could feel my face boiling. They probably felt the heat of it. "I'll teach you one, so," he says, "from the a to the zee." So we're going down Mount Pleasant Street and he's singing *Girls Were Made To Love and Kiss*, getting me to repeat each line. And they all went in'—he tapped his head— 'first time, back of the net. We get to Willenhall, pull up in my road, and he doesn't let me out till I've sung it through for him—from the a to the zee, like he said.'

A moment later, the music stopped in the pub. The musicians were on a break—or perhaps doing as I was: listening to *Girls Were Made To Love and Kiss*—the full job now, a to zee. His voice didn't waver this time. He was back there, in that long-lost December, among the long-gone factories and shunt yards of the Black Country. I imagined the sodium-lit arterial roads vibrating occasionally to the sparse night traffic. Snow about, or at least a hard frost. The last buses going from one smoky town to another—or were they still trolleys? And in the middle of it, the plush box bowling along, in which there was song, geniality, laughter, in which a dream was coming true. I even imagined myself there, mischievous as the driver, trying a bit of Buddy Holly. 'Ah, lad, lad,' I imagined Josef Locke saying. 'Spare us the twang-twang.' In my mind, he laughed like a drain.

The rendition closed to applause and whistles from the pub, curious faces at the window. It also brought a figure to the edge of my vision. It could have been the one I saw earlier, in the doorway. Without properly looking, I assumed it was one of my impatient crew and dug out my wallet. But then it spoke: 'So, you kiss them when you can, eh?' A smallish, roundish woman stood beside us, her upper body all but hidden by a cavernous shoulder bag. Her eyes twinkled at Mr Robbins, who grinned back broadly, still the fourteen- or fifteen-year-old sliding into the Bentley in Marchant Street. 'As long as they're you,' he chuckled.

'Private booking, is it?' she asked, twinkling at me.

'Something like that.' It was the first time I'd said anything.

But Mrs Robbins was now attending to her husband: 'Come on, love,' she said affectionately, 'you'll be overdoing it. It's getting packed out in there. Here's your jacket.' She arranged it round his shoulders; a sober grey muzzled the riot of his shirt. 'We can have a nightcap at the hotel. And there's the session in Ennistymon tomorrow—more music for you.'

Mr Robbins winked at me: 'What can I do but obey?' He held out a hand. Once again it was shivering: 'Thank you for your company,'

'Thank you for the song.'

'Did all right, didn't I?'

'From the a to the zee,' I said, bidding them goodnight. As they slowly disappeared along the street, I heard a voice at the back of my neck. Not, alas, Josef Locke's.

'Next round's definitely yours,' it announced. 'Even if we have to sell you for it.'

Without thinking, I opened my wallet, peeled off some notes and passed them over my shoulder. 'Just a half for me.'

'There's seventy here!' The voice, so cheerily emphatic a moment before, was faint with disbelief.

'Set them up for the session folk. And ask if they'd do *The Desert Song.*'

'Jig, is that?'

Briefly, my songster and his wife were illuminated by a newsagents' night-light.

'Just ask them.'

Footsteps retreated behind me. After a minute or two, the squeezebox cantered into that song of brave farewells, foes anticipated—and girls again. Fiddle, guitar and mandolin swung in behind it. Deftly, a whistle began embroidering the tune. I stayed put, watching the Bentley's passenger of honour and his twinkling wife till they were just beyond the last lamp of the street. The waiting darkness played tricks with her bag. It seemed to

64

swell, and I fancied that duo had become trio: that Josef Locke was squiring them home, testing his ill but ardent acolyte on his whole repertoire, from the a to the zee.

First published in *Staple New Writing—issue 72—Winter 2009/Spring 2010*

One Is One

The bird, there, right in the middle of the field. It didn't move—well, it did a bit, enough to show that it was alive. Its wings fanned a little, its head twitched. I looked away a minute and when I looked back it was over the trees. So it could fly. I couldn't believe it: was tempted not to but that was to be expected. It happens: you think you see what you want to see. I've played myself false that way before now, with other things. But it was there all right. They hadn't all gone, then, the birds.

It's the quiet, really. That took some getting used to. When I was a boy and we'd be on holiday, some remote place, one of the family would say *Isn't it quiet?* And it would be. None of that engine rumble at the edge of the day. *Isn't it dark?* was another one. You'd see a few lights at night, scattered, minding their own, but it wasn't town-night, not that sodium mist all across the horizon like bombs frozen just as they go off. Now it's all quiet and dark like that. Now everywhere is remote.

The animals are doing all right. To begin with you'd have thought they'd go berserk, be at each other's throats, driven by the sudden need to reconfigure the food chain. Bulls and dogs, I thought: bulls and dogs would be the ones to stake their claim at the top, along with anything that managed to quit the zoos. And sometimes, in the distance, you hear a flare-up of barks and growls, but then it stops again. Either they're quick killers or defending their territory or just greeting each other after their kind. But I don't think it's the first: I haven't seen any blood or mangling on my travels. As for territory, you don't see the same animals in the same places, either. This can make for surprises—nearly made my heart stop at first, to turn a corner, come face to face: 'Shouldn't you be behind bars?' I'd think, or 'Shouldn't you be on TV, cantering around places with unpronounceable names?' Conditioning: I'll never be rid of it, I suppose, but it doesn't bother me. Since I see so few physical reminders of back then, memories have become almost physical themselves. It's almost as if, while they're floating through my head, I could pluck them out, set them in my hand like little music boxes. My souvenirs. Well, lighter to carry than a lot of bits and bobs.

They don't bother me, the animals, don't bother with me. They just look—not quite through you but with the merest brush of awareness that you exist. 'Oh, one of you,' they seem to say. A bit like what you used to see in people's eyes, town centre, home-time, buses and jams. You'd be caught in their vision for a flickery second, then dropped because, well, they have a place to go and a thing to do, just as you did, looking back at them the same way. Buses and jams, lights, sirens, home-time. More bits and bobs in the head.

Cars are funny. They're the exotic animals now. You see them in the oddest places. One was in the middle of a field. That's partly why I did a double-take when I saw that bird. I'll look away, I thought, and when I look back it'll be another sad little car gone as far as it can go and now at peace among the green. Back before, you might have called it art, someone's idea about dumping technology in Mother Nature's lap. And sometimes it is

67

plain comical. One car I saw at the top of a ridge: a sporty job, flash and filigree, like you'd have seen barrelling down a hairpin pass in an advert, open-top, pretty people, freedom and sex, always on open road, nothing in front or behind, nothing coming the other way. When did this country ever have such roads? Well, it does now, of course, everywhere.

But this car on the ridge, it was perched on its underside, that's how narrow the ridge was. I was down below a bit and I worked my way over from side to side. Front and back, its wheels were touching nothing. You'd have thought a giant car-stork had let go its sling overhead, dropped the poor baby smack on the spine of the ridge. Nobody in there. Nobody in any cars I've come across, but that's how it was. The cars knew first. They came thundering out of garages, in conga-lines down multi-storey levels, out of supermarket car parks. They knew, and they tried to get as far as they could while they could. But then…perhaps that car on the ridge was driving at the sky. Beyond the blue horizon, eh? Isn't that how the song goes? Beyond the blue horizon waits a beautiful day.

I was in a place much like this when the cars tried to escape. An evening road, I recall, lush verges—just walking along. A car came screaming towards me. I might not have noticed anything—well, you know, country roads, hotheads making the most of a bit of space, pretending to be in one of those adverts. But there was a sharpish left bend where I'd got to so I could see right into the car and it was empty. I didn't think about the logistics of it all: a car driving itself, getting faster though the road was starting to climb so nothing to do with momentum. Life, that's all I thought of, and whether I could throw myself deep enough into the hedge to hang onto it. But the car swung with the bend and raced past, still screaming. I mean, screaming. Not over-revving, not the whine of going flat out in low gear. Screaming with fear, human fear.

Later, when I thought back on it, when I had a second to think with everything else going on, I actually wasn't that surprised. Humans made cars; hand-crafted or born by the hour on assembly lines, cars got to know their creators. Small wonder, then, that they became human themselves in some way: all that exposure to banter, anxieties, frustrations. Like they used to say about old churches, how the stones absorbed all the millions of prayers and something of those who prayed them. You can't blame the cars—if I'd been one, I'd have tried to get out sharpish and I wouldn't have waited for humans to leap in me. I'd have known that what was happening was all about them. Why give a ride to a problem when you can leave it in the dust?

I'm no omega man. You see the odd person here and there. To begin with it was like you'd expect: eyes shining suspicion in the dusk, movement of hands into pockets for something to attack or defend with. But it was just gestures, and anyway, it's always one to one. There are no packs of feral survivalists. Maybe there were, and maybe some of the heftier animals set aside their new unconcern and dealt with them. I can just imagine it, the beasts of the field walking away after, turning once to look back, thinking, that'll learn you,

69

shoe on other foot and all that. Feral survivalists. Films about the future were full of them. Always that scenario, dystopias every which way. Well, it made for good box office: what's to come is what's to fear. Just think of all the films pumping out that message in a trillion cinemas, deep into all those heads. Abuse, really, an imposed disablement. Shake in your boots and carry on. Trust those who lead. They know how to sound like they know. Dystopias. One of the many cons back then.

When I meet someone, we keep things to a minimum. If one of us looks in a bad way, sure, the other will help. But no-one really does. Whoever I meet just looks a little woozily surprised, as though they've just woken up and the first thing they see is me. No doubt I look the same. We keep things light: how are you doing? Shoes holding out? Good berrying round here, good leaves? But there are unspoken rules. We never say 'Have you seen anyone else?' It's a kind of fancy that—telepathically, you might say—we remind each other to stick to: the notion that we're the only two and when we've spoken we'll be on our separate ways and we'll make out however we make out and good luck to you, all the best. Things feel safer that way.

One thing we always swap, though, is where we were when it happened. One jolly lad was in the back of a car with a woman who wasn't his girlfriend. Naturally, the car came to life, handbrake-turned, flung them out and gunned it. They just lay there all crumpled and stunned. That is, he did:

'Not the foggiest idea where she went. Just me face down with my pants all askew. I got up, looked about,

70

called. Thought she might have clung onto the car but she'd have needed to be a proper leech to do that. No sign—and she'd been wrapped round me like a bloody poultice.'

I was out for one of my walks, like I said, when that empty car came haring past. Alone when it happened. A sad feeling for a while, gut-pinching. But, as it turned out, the best preparation.

I like to keep my voice in trim. Nothing better than strolling along, orating to the day. I say orating but I keep it low: still early days, after all, and despite what I've seen, how things are turning out, you still have to be careful. I have a bit of fun, putting on different accents, reeling through all the phrases that meant nothing and led nowhere: *systemic failure, lessons have been learned, we shall instigate a full review, the good of the nation, the good of the community, the good of the people, people, people...* You could say I'm a custodian. I have a care for the words, I pity them their maltreatment, chained in phrases like that. I try to give them the meaning they were always denied. If I say, *at the end of the day,* it always is at the end of the day, when the light's tiring and I'm looking for a place to turn in. I found a bunch of stationery at the roadside once, no doubt from a fleeing van. Between a wad of paper was an envelope. I gripped it hard at either end and said what I was doing out loud as I did it. Not too hard, though; it was a nice one, cream, good quality, a bit like they used to use for deeds and wills. I've still got it. It might come in useful.

What that man said about his disappearing girl. It made me think about the Bible, the rapture, that prediction that all the good folk would be scooped up from the earth before the end of days did for the rest. I'm no scholar, no expert on anything: big pictures in a primary school *Life of Jesus,* a vicar who always ended his phrases with 'um'—'Our Fatherum, Which art in Heavenum'—that's all I remember on the faith side. But I'm just wondering if it hasn't happened arse-about. That things are trying to get back to what they were, so all the *systemic failure* merchants have been…what? Sucked into a fiery pit? De-moleculed? It's just a theory—hardly that. And it seems hard lines on someone like that girl flung from the car. Perhaps I'll meet a theologian, a vicar, and they can fill me in, slip me the word. Unless they've all been…well, like I say, I'm just puttering round the edges of it right now.

Towns and cities I keep clear of. I suppose that much in the dystopian films was right. Not that I have any hard reason to—it's nothing I've seen, experienced. The odd few people I've met, they weren't country-folk. When we trade tales of where we were when it happened, they weren't sitting pretty on a hayrick or worrying about a fallow field. Then again, they weren't all sagging and breathless, hotfoot from some metropolitan hell-hole. When it all happened, I expected to see streams of maddened townies at large upon the land, kitchen knives aloft, laying hold of everything from squirrels to Herefords. But no. I did wonder if they'd all stayed put and were troughing on each other, or maybe the reverse-rapture had exploded them along with all the spokesmen and advisors and what-have-you. I went to the edge of a town one day. Silent. I went back the same night. Silent and dark. Streets empty, curtains still, nothing whizzing past my ear, or worse. There was one sound, like a saucepan lid sliding off. An open window somewhere, maybe, a kitchen where someone was just in the act of checking the veg when it happened and didn't have time to replace the lid. Didn't have time to remember lid, kitchen, street, world. Or maybe a gazelle was ambling about, knocking against something with its…flank, is it? If I'm honest, I never bothered with those nature programmes on TV. I'm making up for it now, of course, for real. So the towns and cities might be ok. It's just one to watch, for now.

One fear I have. It woke me a few nights back, got me out of someone's abandoned bed and up at their abandoned window. A parakeet, I thought, a cockatiel floating about across the moon. I think that must have planted in my mind the hope that the birds hadn't all gone, which was why I was so happy to see the one in the middle of the field. A parakeet, I told myself, a cockatiel. A peacock? That kind of hard, air-tearing sound. I prayed it wasn't a claxon, a trumpet: the announcement that, even now, there was someone out there with, God help us, a plan, an advisor who had, say, dodged the rapture-cull and was set on rounding up anyone who was left so that they—he—could lay new footings, place the foundation stone for cementing in, start on the new…the old…the same old…

That's the one thing that troubles my journeying: that the blue sky, the quiet water, the lazing clouds, the own-business-minding dogs and cheetahs will instantly be megaphoned out of existence by some hand-me-down

Caesar. Who begat Charlemagne. Who begat Napoleon. Who begat…

First published in *Theaker's Quarterly Fiction #50—Spring 2015*

The Portswick Imp

She.

You want a bike, you buy a bike. There's shops all over the place. You look in the window, you go in, you find the bloke and he finds spanners and stuff for the seat and the handlebars so you can try some out. You buy or you come back later or you go elsewhere. And they're all there together: wheels, frame, saddlebag if you like. The bloke doesn't have to go hunting for the bits and fixing them up. Look, here's one takes your fancy, nicely adjusted, balls of your feet on the floor when you mount. I'll have it delivered, you say. I'll ride it away now. Not without paying, you add. Chuckles. And there it is. I told him, there it is. Told him and told him.

He.

Jennifer Workman said she'd bring it back by the weekend, then the next weekend, then the next. Mum somehow pretended patience, and anyway she had the car for work. But she liked a ride out on her bike, and Dad had spent so much time getting it as good as new. And I'd helped: well, I'd stood by with the oil and the spanners like a star mechanic, waving them about, fixing invisible bike after bike in the air, till I noticed that Dad had shifted round on his kneeler and was giving me his *I'm waiting* look. Then I'd hand him the oil when he wanted a spanner or vice versa. We'd have a good laugh at that. I would. Mum did the last flourishes: white line on the crossbar, all along the crown of the mudguard. Not a shake, dead calm, she could have been using a ruler. She never didn't.

I said to him, look, we could just buy two bikes and go off together. Or Tricia's bike would be fine for me. I can't see her suddenly wanting it to be shipped over to Winnipeg. She didn't even take it to uni. And last time Davey was home, I said, he was on about getting a motorbike, so he'd probably be giving his up, he could bring it back for you, God knows that tank he drives has enough room for half-a-dozen pushbikes in the back. So ask him, I said. Ask him. Talk about talk to yourself.

Jennifer Workman had form. Dad had to give the mower's engine the kiss of life when she brought it back and Mum swore up and down the slow cooker didn't make that sound before she borrowed it. I'll bring the bike back next weekend, then the next—on the phone she said it, on the doorstep, once clear across the shopping centre. The weekends came and went, we did family things, William and Jane kept annoying me. Still no bike. I used to ask Mum why she'd gone and had twins. She just laughed. She had a certain laugh when she spoke about them or to them. Not like the laugh she used to me. Longer, deeper, her laugh for them. I guessed it had to be because there were the two of them. It had to last.

Tell you the truth, I thought it was cars he'd get into when Tricia and Davey left home. He used to go on about his mom's cars, his dad's vans. You'd think they were Queenie's Balmoral run-arounds, the way he described them. They didn't strike me as special. The dad's were death-traps, each worse than the last. That grey one, I could hardly bring myself to get in it, but get in it I had to, one time, family picnic, those twins and all. You'd say it came out of the Ark except there couldn't have been two of them in all this world. There was a funny snouty thing on the dash: 'trafficator', he and the dad said together. You weren't to call it an indicator. So that's how old the thing was. No floor-shift, no stuffing in the seats, near enough. But as long as you said 'trafficator', that'd make everything right, like St Christopher used to before he got laid off. That'd protect you against rain, wind and weather, except it didn't, worst picnic I've known, hunched up with that petrol smell, the mother's elbow in my ear when she reached for another sandwich and where she got those cups I'll never know.

A semi-thief, really, Jennifer Workman. That's how it looked on that Saturday. We'd been out all day and when we got back, there Mum's bike was, propped half-out of the back gate. Heaven knows how long it had been there just asking to be pinched. Not that anyone would have, not with the state it was in. Dad's lovely emerald paintwork, the fussy white lines, all gone. Almost. You could make out a stretch of white on the cross-bar, underneath the tar. That's how thick the black paint was, that's what showed she must have had Heaven's own scrape with it. All down the saddle post as well, and I'd spent an afternoon sanding the rust off that before Dad let me splash a bit of oil round the base when he got properly to work on it—like I was christening a ship.

Black tar, still drying. Of course, William and Jane had to get their hands all over it. Mum laughed and hurried them away, singing her song about washing your hands in orange juice, the pair of them joining in. She had songs for when they tumbled or had the sulks or dropped their food. She found her voice with them.

Dad got a couple of old rags and a spanner and pulled the bike away from the gate. He tried loosening the saddle post, turning it round and back, but all he got for his pains was a goitre of black where it met the frame.

'I'm not sure,' he said, 'that it's really your mother's.'

I pointed out the stretch of white, but he said everyone and their dog had lines like that on their bike.

'Would have been more stylish if she hadn't bothered.'

He didn't sound like he was talking to me.

Neither hide nor hair of Jennifer Workman after that, though Mum said she saw her the following week outside Miss Le Manquis' house with bits of a Dutch airer.

Champagne taste on a beer budget, him and cars. You'd think we weren't starting out, you'd think two kids under three didn't need so much as a bib, that they were happy to take themselves off and sweep chimneys. For a while we had one of the dad's leavings, a van he'd half-destroyed to get side windows in, crank hole and no crank handle. After that, it all started. We got a Rover, he preferred an Escort; so, all right, an Escort, and he prefers a Carmen Ghia, whoever made those—sounded like that singer who stored fruit in her hair. On it went, through the Vauxhall, the Citroen, you name it. Another week, another handbook. All that time and we never owned a car outright. Maybe one. For a month. And him always leaving the showroom backwards, ogling what he still really wanted, jangling the keys to the choice we'd held him to, me and his bank manager. Davey picked up that routine from him. Exam after exam, he'd come home saying he'd done question 2a and should have done 2b. Tricia did all right with a third-hand Clio for years.

And then the Mini fixation. Let me lay it out for you: boy of sixteen, girl of fourteen, me and him and shopping and holiday suitcases and all the usual teenage bits and dabs and fisticuffs. Imagine all that stuffed in a Mini. I had God's own job to wean him off that notion. Much later we all had to cram into Tricia's Clio when we visited her at uni. 'This is what it would have been like,' I said, 'with a Mini. Coffin on wheels.' Tricia laughed like a drain, or would've, only I had to cut her off, all that noise in her little cube, God help my hearing. Davey said Minis were cool, which is hardly the gun he's stuck to, him and those Land Cruisers he goes in for. Land Chewers, more like. Whenever he parks in front of our house it's an eclipse, we need the lights on.

His nibs said nothing. He looked to be the only one with a bit of space round him. Probably shrank himself to make a point.

Mum never rode her bike after that. I took it over— managed to push the handlebars and saddle down through all that dried gunk. Alright, it was a woman's bike but that didn't fuss me. Dad and I, we'd worked on it together. Then William and Jane got twin bikes,

79

stabiliser jobs, and I was instructed to take them out in the park, get them up and running, confident.

There wasn't much in the way of biking for me with all of that. Stop and start, checking William's seat, unclogging the streamers Jane insisted on. It got to me: time after time with all that freedom to hand and me quarantined on a patch of ratty grass. So one day, when they'd got past the no-tears stage and were following each other's tails in a wobbly circle, I took off, did my old circuit, every hill in reach, ending with a skid-swing into the service drive that ran alongside the main road. If I got up enough steam, I could take that drive without pedalling, legs out in a V if I wanted. And I did want, then, and I did it.

Of course, the park was deserted when I got back. There was a houseful of sobs and thunder and 'Your Dad, your Dad, you wait.' Jane had apparently been so frantic she flew like a banshee back along our street, streamers aloft, a shrieking target for any car door flung carelessly open. There were no cars parked in the street, just Miss Le Manquis' Traveller, which wasn't going anywhere, one tyre down, gobbets of oil under the grille. No point, though, my saying that. The point was the earful I got, embellished that night by Dad who reminded me that he'd been the big brother too and spoke of responsibility and how it was high time I got myself looked up to.

The bike disappeared not long after. I stood in the park as, bit by bit, the streamers and stabilisers came off. For a while I took to walking my old route, feeling how strange it was to be plod-plodding through the spaces I'd torn up with speed. It almost felt as though the house fronts reproached me, as though the service drive said, *well, well—reduced to this?* But all that passed. I struck my terms with the ground, though sometimes I'd go misty and get God's own spurt on, till I came out of it and my mates were in a heap half a street behind, laughing their socks off. I never asked for another bike. Never looked at one.

A week, maybe, after Tricia emigrated? Yes, so about a month after Davey got the job in Stroud. We'd had the Laguna about a year. Comfiest car we'd ever had, but oh, I thought, here we go, the old, old story. He starts gawping about in bad traffic, lingering on clear roads, the number of times we got pipped and flashed, it was embarrassing. I thought, yearning for a Bentley now are we? But that wasn't it. The to-do he made of passing cyclists, pulling right out like he wanted to cruise the hedge opposite, gawping again as he got round. I wouldn't say her bum was worth all that, I thought, or hers, or hers. But that wasn't it either.

It came back like an old song. I realised that, deep down, I must have had an eye on them always. The way they flashed among the cars, the way they seemed to know which alleys to duck down to get out of the chaos, even if their owners didn't. The way a pair of them danced on the road ahead: abreast, then the one slowing and tucking in behind the other so that was all you really saw, one back tyre and one pair of legs with maybe just a shade of something else in front. The two of them throwing air over either shoulder.

81

Once a bloke cycled across the park near us on the main pathway (a proper park, this one, bandstand and tended flowers). I watched him stop, feet down, one hand still on the bar. He looked up and around, listened to the birds I was hearing, shaded his eyes and studied a cloud above us, big and wide, curving clear to the next town. He jerked the handlebar like reining in a horse, like I used to, and I thought he was going to haul it right back and go hell for leather up to that fat cloud road. But he saw me instead and grinned, sheepish, and we exchanged the time of day as you do in an awkward moment—no words, just *Orra? Orra*—and on he went. I stayed stock still, the sorcerer's apprentice messing up a beautiful spell. He'd have done it if I hadn't been there. Straight up into that cloud. Sure he would.

You want a bike, you buy a bike, and you don't get it in bits from all over England. I stopped going with him in the end. Tricia and Davey off being purposeful and needed, and here I was stumping about scrap yards after his nibs. Always in the rain, too, and all these places have corrugated roofs. What with that and him dislodging piles of metal, thrusting his hands under rods and spokes, it was like gunfire. 'Ah, this might suit', he'd say, and our car would be down on its axles with a pile of frames, mudguards, handlebars from racers, sit-up-and-beg jobs.

I stopped going to the dank shops, too, each with its mumbly little man in a brown coat stuffed with pens. The two of them would slide into the back and make noises at each other with the odd name popping out. There was some kind of pecking order. Rudge or Raleigh, they sounded like dogs with mouths full of sausages. Freddie Grubb and Claude Butler made the two of them sound like his mum when she saw my outfit for our wedding, all sniffy and if-you-must-you-must. Philips got a little chorus of approval; Schwinn (I think it was) made me think they were having a nail-spitting contest.

And away he'd come with leaflets and plans, just like his dad, another bumf-merchant. I'd wander round out front, always the only one there, nose full of oil and touch-up paint. Once I clattered into a bike strung up from a beam. A beauty, it was, even I could tell that, and you didn't need to lift it down to see that it would do him just right.

'There's one here,' I called. 'Perfect.'

I don't know what the silence of the moon is like but I'll bet it wasn't far off what I got. Then one of them gave a slow covering cough, a fart-in-church effort, and the sausage-scoffing and nail-spit noises started up again.

Dad first, then Mum, and her funeral was the last time I saw William and Jane. The traffic was bad and they were just finishing the first hymn when we arrived. I started to lead us up the aisle, weathering the embarrassment, till I got a dig in the back.

'I wouldn't bother,' she says. And I saw that the front two rows were crammed and there was nothing for us. But Davey and Tricia were teenagers, so it was just as well we retreated to the back. The view was restricted, though I could see my brother and sister in the middle of their broods, shoulders back, sitting up and begging like they'd done through all those days going round and round in the ratty park. Not a squeak out of their kids. They'd been taught their circles.

The do afterwards was on the terrace of a country hotel, which wasn't what I'd agreed to at all. By that time she was getting as bolshie as Davey and Tricia. Not that I could blame her, or them.

Then Jane's youngest wheedled the car keys from her mum and reappeared with a bike the spit of Jane's ratty park job. No streamers but a pennant hooked behind the saddle: *Princess On Board.* Round the terrace she looped, catching a skirt or two, clattering a table. Then her Uncle William whispered something and she made for us, circling round and round where we stood. This caused general chuckles, largely of relief I should think, since she wasn't menacing anyone else's clothes. William and Jane were staring straight at me, hemmed in as I was by a Princess for whom 'look at this' was understood.

Funny pair, those twins. Wouldn't be your first choice for brother- and sister-in-law. July, now, or August, that's the time for outdoors, not windy old April. Mind you, you can drink more without folk clocking it than you can in a room. And that takes your mind off the weary sandwiches. I was that close to giving Jane's little loony a cuff. One splash of oil on my skirt and she'd have been freewheeling into hospital. Bugger of buggers, oil, especially on pink. I don't know what that routine was all about, whizzing round and round us. Maybe I'd let slip sometime about how he'd never done a hand's turn helping ours to ride. That'd be just like them, using one of their kids to make a point. Finally Davey kicked her

84

rear wheel and she was off back to mommy and it was all blubs and tut-tuts. I didn't tell Davey off. Neither did he. Well, he was halfway back to the car by then.

It took God's own age to find just that shade of emerald. That shop where she called out, saying she'd found just the bike for me, the chap promised he could get some in by next week, which came and went with all the other weeks. Jennifer Workman all over again. In the end I tracked some down in a hobby shop, tiny pots, a stack of them. So there I was: like doing the Forth Bridge with a toothbrush.

But it was worth it. The whole thing looked a treat. The colour sort of welded all the different bits together, all five bikes' worth. Three-speed, naturally, and I ordered a metal badge, too, for the front post, and a chap I knew got a chap he knew to work it up, bordering, design, red against the emerald, name in the middle, how he did what he did in that small space, I tip my hat. Of course, Dad was that way, handy as you like. And, fair's fair, he tried with me. I'd have loved to ride it up into the sky like that bloke was set to do that day in the park, seek Dad out in his shiny white district and say, here, Dad, look. Look.

Some harbour strike, I think, in the Sixties. The news was on while we were having our tea and the newscaster was talking in that adult ball-throwing way, over my head and into Mum's and Dad's: 'Of all the ports, Wick is least affected.' The two words gummed themselves together, a gift of mishearing—like Our Father who art in heaven, Harold be thy name. I never forgot, so of course it went smack in the middle of the badge. Portswick. The Portswick Imp.

I got cuffed by a teacher once. We were the first junior class to get a mobile blackboard and I was mesmerised by the space behind it. It was an extra bit of the room, free of us, our messes and wrong answers: a magic land, bound to be. So I slipped round the board in the middle of a lesson and got slipped back out again smartish.

'Where on earth do you think you're going?'

'Miss, I'm going to Portswick.'

Dad laughed fit to burst at that. Mum sighed, then went back to her oogy-googy chat with the twins, what a pudd'n your brother is, what a soggy pudd'n, don't grow up that way, eh, oogy-goog?

The Imp bit was a nod to all the Goblins, the Sprites, the Varsities that made life sweet back then. If I'd been allowed to go to Portswick, one of them would have sped out of thin air and taken me on the parcel rack. And it was a nod to me. I'd been an imp, too, sneaking behind that board.

I didn't bother with white lines. The emerald was perfect.

I'll have an affair, I said. I'll open my door to the meter-man. Didn't make a ha'porth of difference. I'll come out with you, I said, look, Tricia's bike is still fine, well, ok-ish, a good wash and buff. I can still manage it, did it enough when I taught her, taught Davey. All on my own-ee-o, I didn't add.

But no. I was the bike-widow. Season come, season

go, off he wobbled. God, you could hear the thing grating and creaking till the turn of the crescent. The days got shorter and he clamped some museum pieces front and back. You'll get stopped with those lights, I said, road safety these days, they're not into candles. Wobble, creak, wobble, creak. Where he went, how far, he never said. Just brought the smell of the world back with him: parkland, tar, the cold of the night. For a moment, there, he'd stand in the house with outside the house all over him. Why Portswick Imp? I said. Because that's where I've been. Odd-bod Street, more like. For a while I thought he was stalking, flashing even, indulging what he hadn't shown me for years. But no-one phoned, no copper left his boot marks in the hall. Wobble, creak.

I was just cruising up to the crown of a hill and the whole town was below me: church, high street, roundabouts, a lake way off beyond. No one driving up or down. Balls of the feet on the ground, hands light and sure on the bars. A pat of the badge, a slight sway to feel the whole thing under me. Tilt and one foot on the pedal. Up and over the crown, a dab of brakes to prepare, to savour: even a wobble because a wobble is what you burst out of to find your line, your gulley of fleetness, with angel hands to pull you on. And down, down, and fast, faster.

And the car, I said, isn't it due a service? That whining's back. He just shrugged.

Sound becoming light becoming wind, chimes though the church is dark, neon and flash though the shops are shuttered, stickmen on the pavements with their effortful steps, dragging along the ground, their eyes never more than a few sad feet above it. Roundabouts, and you go down deep on the outside, tilt like on a motorbike, but gentler, more feathery, push-bikes can just drop away from you if you're not careful. Double roundabouts are a joy, you can swerve north-west with your eye north-east, keep the speed, too, you'd be surprised, you can wishbone your legs when you're back on the straight, even get a hand out at full stretch.

Horseradish. First time I met his mother, just about her first word. Loves horseradish, she said, whatever meat he's having, or not. I thought it was one of those little homilies to show she'd always know him best: dropping a note for the future. Except she kept trotting it out, and the odder the occasion, the more she went on about it. Crowded restaurant, tour bus, naturally our wedding reception. When her funny twins were old enough she'd say it straight to them and the three of them'd share their special laugh, overlong, meant to be cute but really creepy. Is that where he's off in the evenings, I wondered, digging up radish beds?

Now up comes the lake with a cinder path round it, which you might stick to, might not, depends if you want to be reminded, circles and circles, ratty park, kid causing grief on a hotel terrace, streamers from a saddle, bugger that, you're your own streamer, what else should you be? And there's Mum at the waterside, turned away from you, riffling in her bag.

Never asked for horseradish all the time I knew him.

Faster, closer, your hand still at full stretch. Mum still turned away, oblivious. This could get you ten points, twenty points—bonanza.

I couldn't tell you where it was. All I can remember is that the sign for the last village was in English and Welsh. Out of the blue after weeks of our usual plodding. I looked him up and down. Why you asking? Think I don't have other things to do? Forgotten how to drive, have you? We're not stopping at one of your little friends' shops on the way, are we? Got on my lungs, all that oil and damp.

Oh…come on, then. I regretted saying it at once. Faff, faff with the bike rack, and the church bells clanging away the time. Look, soon be dark, I said. Faff, faff. Stuff this, I'm going in, Davey's calling by in the morning on his way to Leeds, bet you've forgotten that, too, I'll need…but then he turned and looked at me and I was all at once everything I'd ever been, mother, lover, angel, bitch, as though he'd pushed our whole life as one picture in through my eyes and held the back of my head till the picture set firm. First time he'd ever looked as though he really knew me.

Over this bridge, he was saying by the time I finally got all that out of my head, then second left. And there we were.

You sure this hill is high enough for you? Twice I said that, once after I'd dug out an extra cardy, once after I'd zipped my fleece. He stood there straddling his pal, his Imp, like there was a Royal Bicycle Corps and he was in it and they were being snapped on parade. Do you want me to drive down and find you or are you coming back up? I said that twice, too, the second time with my hand on his shoulder. Look, should I put Davey off? Tomorrow?

He said nothing, just started working the wheels back and forth. Aren't you freezing? I said. God knows where that shirt came from, I'd never seen it before, the cut of it, Lord help us, talk about Dennis the Menace, probably filthy dirty, and I was just leaning to have a sniff of it when all of a sudden there was just me with my hand open to the cold.

You can trace the point where everything stops being alright. So you can trace the point just before it. That's always there, however far off you've ridden from it, in whatever direction, however many faces get in the way, whatever their game is. I'm closing in on my just before, though it looks so different now. It's this drop in front of me, that bend, the rise as gentle as they say love is, the pull to the left and…I can't see after that. Don't need to. For that bloke that time in the park, it was the sight of the cloud-road over our heads. But I got in his way. *Orra?* he said, embarrassed, and I said it too and I confined him to the earth. So this is for him as well. I'm off to Portswick, Miss.

His head stayed clear as anything even with the light going. A dot among the trees below then up along a meadow, then a twist and gone. Bells in the distance there, too, drumming the hours into my body where I stood and stood. After however long I thought I saw his funny lights wobbling back but it was just a bit of the Welsh moon broken up.

'Starting trouble?' Farmer-type, I'd say, off home in the wee small hours, and I pretended yes, and he got a torch and squinted and probed and couldn't see anything, till, 'Well, try her again.' I had paper, he had a pen, couldn't hardly read his writing, just relied on his arrows and a big X for the main road. I got home just about Tricia's suppertime. Our voices came and went on the phone, each turn with its little gap saying thousands, thousands of miles.

'Police?' she suggested.

And it sounded absurd, like one of those words long out of use in a brainbox game on TV. Clairvoyant? she might as easily have said. Ghost hunter? And, fair dos, she must have realised. So I just sat on and we listened to each other's silence.

God knows how long…but I guess she'd hung up, it was daylight and Davey was putting the receiver back and taking my hand in his, leaning forward. He didn't say anything. And the birds didn't trill and the letterbox didn't clatter and the phone didn't ring and the gate didn't slam and I could have popped the ring on my wedding finger in two, like a tiny bleb of oil.

Give You A Game?

It was the scarf. They said the desk had been cleared but a bit of dirty-looking tartan still poked out under the lid. The desk had been moved to the side of the classroom but with its back to the wall, so you could still sneak a glance at the scarf. During the last day of term, he found it harder and harder not to.

'Away with the fairies again, Paul?' Mrs Watton's voice wasn't unkind, hadn't been at any time throughout the year. Without resentment, Paul turned back to his book. But he still saw the scarf like a pattern behind the words he read, and his heart was still on fire.

The kids scattered at the summons for tea. Once it was issued, front windows were slammed all along the street. Two brothers wrestled at their gatepost to see who'd be first to shoulder the back door off its hinges and forget to wash his hands. One boy, as usual, had to be called three times.

Only Paul was left, looking down at his shoes and the small ridges in the concrete road, wondering if the press of his feet had made the road go like that. From an open window somewhere came the song everyone was singing or sending up. Someone saw someone else's love yesterday and she told them what to say. Say-ee-yay. It seemed to Paul that the flock of *Yeah, yeah, yeahs* made the day very different, like strange birds on the roof tiles. I could fly away with them, he thought.

A horn sounded and he turned to see Mr Phillips's Ford Anglia, light-green, nipped little angles. Smiling, Mr

Phillips gestured that Paul might like to step aside. The car crept past and Mr Phillips gave him the kind of wave that Mrs Watton had given him earlier that day, at the end of the school year. He'd seen his mum doing something not dissimilar, when they were seeing off some relatives at the station. Vaguely he supposed that it was one of the many things he'd be doing sometime. Adult things. A special energy would flow into his hand when he reached an age he couldn't imagine, and before he knew it he'd be waving with assurance in clothes he'd chosen himself. But he couldn't see himself getting to that.

What next? He had no idea. There'd be tea, yes, but his mum wasn't long back. The kids had had to make way for her car just before play broke up; it'd be a bit longer before she called him. But after tea? He'd never felt like this before: simply moved without thought in the unslipping hula hoop of friends, school, records, evening play, holiday exultation. Hadn't he just been shouting and tackling with the best of them? But in the middle of it he'd sort of gone elsewhere. He'd gone on charging about with the others but he sensed that, at any moment, their arms and legs would cut right through him as if he were just a bit of afternoon heat their efforts had troubled.

His mum was pretty brisk. Presently he'd hear his name, once: she wasn't really a street-shouter, preferring to add 'It's stone-cold' in the kitchen if he was late. Still, best walk towards that single call. But he couldn't move—no, he could but was scared of what might happen. I put out one foot, he thought, then the other, then the first. But what then? Where do I go? He pictured the house front to which his efforts should take him. Somehow he didn't trust that they would and for a second he wondered if the house existed. 'My house,' he murmured. It sounded as unlikely as the bit of French his uncle had tried to teach him. *Je touche le tableau noir.* I touch the blackboard. Bonkers. Why make strange noises when you said you were going to touch and the blackboard was what you'd be touching? But 'My house' sounded strange, too. All that business of making air and twisting your mouth round it. If someone was in front of him right now and he said it, would they understand?

All the others. He envied how they'd made their bee-lines when tea was called. Natural sprints and swerves, no need for thought. He'd done the same before today. But now he was thoughtful, though not in the way people meant it (stupid words again, twisting about when they should make steady sense). Thoughts were all over his mind like butterflies trapped in a room. Inviting him—daring him?—to cup them in his hands, even one, and get a good look. Some of them trailed something, vapour, a shadow, like the start of a clue, a way in. Like a scarf hanging from a desk lid.

'All right, Paul?' Mr Phillips, now out in his front garden, waved. 'Thought you'd test my brakes back there?'

Paul waved back. The butterflies surged as a single arrow. He gave his feet a go, one foot, other foot…it worked but he wouldn't have done it if he hadn't had an audience, a grown-up at that, with a grown-up's assumption that kids liked stillness about as much as bath-time. One thought came clear through the butterflies and probably kept his feet going. After tea—yes, the game again. They'd all be back, he could run right into it in a single move, his bee-line, table to street. The old jumping and diving, new ideas played out along railing and privet, by walls so high they pushed the sky away. That got him to the curve of the road, within sight of his home. But he stalled again. *Je touche le tableau noir.* The picture he'd conjured now seemed as mystifying as that. The butterflies were a snowstorm.

Just one more thing he had to try, though it felt worse than moving his feet. 'All right, Paul?' Mr Phillips had said. How strange his name had sounded, sudden on the air. Like nothing he'd heard before. So now, how about…? Drawing a deep breath, he whispered it to himself, briskly, then stretching it like the gum Mrs Watton was always confiscating from John Muldoon. It didn't sound any friendlier.

A familiar trickling began in the pit of his stomach, ice water, such as he felt at the moment when a difficult sum started to get away from him in class. *If it takes three men five hours to dig a trench two yards wide by…I buy A for one-and-thruppence, B for sevenpence-ha'penny, C for six…* Now he envied the trench-diggers, the talkative shopper. How safe to live in a world where you only have to stick spades in the ground or walk—no, run—about the shops with money spilling from your fingers. He'd go and live with them, dig away and pause only to stock up on chocolate.

'Paul!' His mum. The butterflies parted long enough for him to bend all this strangeness his own way. He was a pilgrim in fog, he imagined, a space buccaneer just landed on a planet whose shapes and colours he didn't recognise. That got him past the curve to the start of the rise.

The nudges came first and then the sniggers. Much elbowing, pointing. You just knew the dirty tartan scarf was on its way, along the railings that joined the school playground to Whitmore Park. You just knew the dirtier coat was trailing after, and the ciggy and, more than once, the slippers. Or the donkey jacket, the plimsolls, the greasy muffler, a ciggy again. Other parents came streaming down Wellington Road or Fraser Street with their children, past the tidy houses with the burnished front steps and razored privet. The scarf, the dirty coat, the donkey jacket issued from the darkness beyond the park, where starlings thronged the black roof of Newbold Brakes and machines belched behind the gates of Wilkinson Packings.

Halfway along Fraser Street, Susan Reilly timed it to perfection, bouncing out of her house, joining the throng but somehow looking as though she were walking in lone elegance. Her mother, head cleaner, was already in the school, loudly supervising a last bit of spit and polish before assembly.

'My mum said she wouldn't use that scarf to wipe our toilet.' More sniggers as countless eyes skewered the tartan. The bright sparks got their usual cries ready, timing them as Susan Reilly timed her launch upon the world.

Parents presented their children at the gates like little

gifts whose shiny footwear would shortly renew tarmac and parquet. Only sometimes was the moment robbed of its lustre by the revving of the cars from which a small group of white-collar heirs emerged. Even Susan Reilly at her stateliest was pushed to match that.

'Hey, Sean!' And the moment had come. At a certain point towards the Fraser Street end of the railings, the dirty coat or donkey jacket turned and retreated, leaving the scarf to slope along on its own.

'Seany! Want me to show you what water looks like?'

'Cooked more sausages for us, Seany?'—this a reference to the scarf-wearer spending a whole lunchtime in the toilet and forgetting to flush.

'How are your pets, Sean Riordan?' Christobel Foulkes was a match for any boy in calling out and all else, though each day found her facing new trouble with keeping her knickers concealed.

'Look, I can see them jumping off his head.'

Laughter and at least one face turning to check if a certain car had been and gone—and, if it had, 'You need to get your mum in here, Paul, with her bag of tricks.'

Christobel's thigh on routine view in a mime of furious scratching: 'One of them's on me already…hey, get off', as a bright spark's hand joined in but went unsmacked.

'Get yer mum, Paul, or we'll itch to death.'

'We'll get measles again.'

'We'll get that spinal biff.'

Paul a little apart, putting on a smile as his serious eyes watched Sean Riordan come through the gates, repelling the last parents like a force field.

'I could live in there.'

Paul's hand traced the bark of the tree by the front wall of Mrs Middleton's bungalow. It was a strange tree, having no kin among the birches or laburnums elsewhere in the road. Its leaves were bluey-lilac, sort of, small and close, like weird snow that had stopped in mid-fall.

'Jacaranda, that,' said his uncle, who'd knocked about a bit. 'Possibly. Or something damn like. Shelter, they need, a spot on the sunny south coast. How it's surviving up here…' A slow shake of the head, such as his uncle delighted in. 'Magic.'

Jacaranda…the kind of name a space buccaneer would give a new planet. He could fold up his ship, stow it in the trunk, shin up the branches and make camp, send signals back to Earth behind the leaves, nice and safe, unspottable. By the time he'd given HQ his readings so the fleet could follow, it would be night and he could slip out, snoop around, send more information. At first light, he'd sort his ship out and return to his forward base, Planet Banyan, a tree whose roots dropped down, said his uncle, like pillars in a church. Prop roots, apparently. He might tell HQ that Jacaranda would be his forward base from now on, that he'd meet the fleet there. Of course he'd have to make dead sure of the Jacaranda terrain so there'd be no nasty—

'Stare at it all you want. It's when the footballs fly into it that I get livid.'

Paul jerked back.

'Hey, don't fall in the road.' Mrs Middleton was

smiling. 'I heard your mum, lad, better cut along.' Waving, she disappeared behind her frost-glass porch.

Paul got out of sight of the bungalow, just, but his feet stalled again.

'All right Da-vid, we saw you qui-ver, kis-sing Margie Fa-llon-down by the ri-ver.'

Squeals.

'How many kisses did you give her altogether…one…two…three…four…'

The rope arcing, two feet hopping in, up-down, four feet, up-down, six feet, a caught ankle, the rope dropped, more squeals. Half a playground away, David Monkton, face burning, cuffing off friends: 'Her fancies you, that Margie.'

'What time is it, Mr Wolf?' John Muldoon hunched against the wall, back to his prey, growling. Christobel Foulkes daintying up in front of the rest, quick glance back, prepared lisp, 'What time is it, Mr Wolf?', a giggle mid-question. John swinging about, arms stretched, prey scattering, Christobel languidly petrified, John grabbing her, 'Harr-arrrrrrrr!'

Spitfires and Stukas, British pilots with American twangs, enemies who could manage nothing more than 'Aaaaieeeee!'

At lunchtime on the last Tuesday of term, Paul was just stepping out of his plane after bombing Foe-land to smithereens. Damn and blast, he'd nearly overshot the runway, which was why he was by the playground wall, far from the rest of the squadron. Clambering gingerly from cockpit to wing to ground, he found Sean Riordan in front of him.

'Ok, Pauly?' Even the act of speaking seemed to stir the smells in his clothes.

Everyone knew the drill. If you were ambushed by the tartan scarf at playtime, you'd make God's own noise to get the herd's attention and then absorb yourself into its safety. All the cat-calling was reserved for the morning arrival, when Sean was put in his same old place for the day. There was no need to waste further words. Once or twice, maybe, someone would cry 'Gyppo!' from the herd's bowels, or John Muldoon would yell something about his big brother and Sean's mum.

But Paul said 'Hey, Sean' now. Sean's eyes widened and immediately he rooted in a pocket.

'Got these.' Two round objects lay in his palm, woody-looking, serrated like duffel buttons.

'My dad got them. Conkers.'

'Conkers? In summer?'

'Magic conkers. Give you a game?' Sean draped two lengths of string over the conkers, ready-knotted.

'I'm in there twice a day,' said Paul's mother in his head, overheard talking to Dad one time when Paul was just off for a street-game. 'Insulin. Poor old lady. The filth of that room. Romancing all the time. Princess Margaret coming to call if you believe her. Says she has a nephew in Paul's class. My eye. Shouldn't think any Riordan's been inside a school.'

Paul had of course never let on about this, but you don't always need words to say stuff. Sean had threaded the first conker.

And all across the playground, something started: a hum with hisses mixed in, the sound of townsfolk when, after biding his time, the mysterious stranger starts the brainwashing. The threaded conker in his hand, Paul turned to see walls of dead blank faces, bodies serving the hiss-hum—louder, louder.

'Get away from him, Paul'—John Muldoon, terror-struck scientist.

'His mum'll have yer'—Christobel Foulkes, never one to miss a chance to be ten years older—'Prozzer!'

And now John Muldoon was inching forward, reaching a hand as though Paul had turned to stone and the ground was breaking up beneath him.

'For pity's sake, man,' he cried, Quatermass-brisk.

The hiss-hum stopped. A knot of bodies parted. John Muldoon was left leaning forward, arm out, a snake-belted, pocket Eros.

'What have you all been told? What have you all been told and told?' In the silence, Mrs Watton walked up behind John Muldoon, reached round and lowered his arm. Sean Riordan kept close to the wall as he ran away. Paul watched him go, expecting him to melt through it, aware of the magic conker still in his hand.

An outstretched arm, a hand flapping. Up the rise, Paul saw the diminutive figure: his younger sister, dispatched in lieu of another reluctant yell from his mum, dumb-showing him to get his skates on. Skates would have been the thing right now—rocket-powered, of course. But he'd left them on Planet Jacaranda. His sister vanished and he got himself up to a couple of yards an hour, for a couple of yards.

'And the gentleman was very angry.' On the last
Wednesday morning of term, the Headmistress paced up
and down the assembly hall. 'Think about your own
houses. Can you see your own houses?'

Nods here and there, a scatter of 'Yes, miss.'

'What do you do in your own houses?'

Something from the middle of the crowd, foolishly
clear.

'All right, John Muldoon, see me after. Now, what do
you do?'

Eat, miss. Play, watch TV. Sleep, miss.

'And you're all safe, yes? You're all safe in your
houses.'

Yeses, mostly.

'And if you fell out of the windows, would you be
safe then?'

A Woodbine-sounding chuckle.

'Bernard Page, with John Muldoon after. Well, would
you be safe?'

'No, miss.'

'No, Christobel, you would not be safe. Just like you
won't be safe if you go through that gap. I've had'—her
fingers got counting—'two telephone calls and then the
gentleman came to see me. From'—chilly and slow—
'the Council. Now it's not just this school. But they have
seen children getting over the boards and through that
gap. We have told you. Told you and told you. If your
parents are not—I repeat, not!—meeting you at four
o'clock, you stay in your groups and you keep to the

102

roads.'

Stepping back, she looked everyone over, row by row.
'Can you all swim?'

Silence.

'Can you? Who cannot swim yet?'

Hands up, about half the hall.

'Exactly. And even if you can, you-stay-in-your-groups-and-you-keep-to-the-roads.'

Paul dragged on, and now the street was frosty and cold. It was last January again and they were getting into Dad's car for Manchester. A second cousin or great aunt or some outlier had…well, Mum was telling Dad that the black was showing up all his dust but then she pulled off her hat and plonked it on her lap, muttered about flipping veils.

For the afternoon, Paul and his two sisters were parked with someone while the adults vanished. There were colouring books and comics, cakes and chat about favourite TV programmes. Paul had brought his own stuff and sat apart, studiously creating a moon colony, thin spiky buildings and monorails overhead. He hadn't a clue what the adults were up to. It sounded like there'd be a lot of them wherever it was, murmuring in that not-for-children subtone they could turn on and off, all in black (barring that ridge of dust on his dad's shoulders). The cousin or great aunt would be there too but not quite in the same way. Moving among them? Not likely. What had happened to her slowed you down, he surmised. But moving nonetheless, perhaps as if on the other side of a window to the rest. On view (his parents had used that phrase) but separate—as you'd be separate from the road, say, if you pushed down those boards and squeezed through.

He blinked. His gate swam up five houses away, and that funny trellis entrance his dad was always about to sort out. Like a lychgate, his uncle said. They'd used such words on the way home, Mum and Dad. And *sombre*, at which his older sister had cried 'Sombrero!' and been shushed. 'Abide with me,' his mom had sighed. He knew what that meant and for a moment had wondered if this cousin or whoever was with them, in the boot.

On Wednesday night, it had turned shivery cold and rained hard. Thursday morning was all fog—crazy for July, but then all the factories and engine yards around didn't need much encouragement to smother everything. Paul's mum had an early call-out—filthy old Granny Riordan maybe—and had offered to drop him and his sisters off at a friend's near the school. Yes, cried the girls, but Paul had seen the adventure in the situation and said he'd catch up with David Monkton and the other knot of boys from round King Street.

Which he didn't try to. This was weird and wonderful, Jacaranda weather, and who knew what he might encounter squawking or tendrilling out of the mists— aside from blokes in peaked caps and mufflers, with snap-tins and Bernard Page's Woodbine cough.

At the top of Loxdale Street, he just made out David Monkton's lanky frame up ahead. Oh, well…he accelerated, only to see that David and another boy were trying to drag each other down a pathway between two

104

houses—

'This is your final hour, Dan Dare!'

'Noooo! Noooo!'

—till a woman appeared from one house and told them to scarper, that there'd been enough trouble and the Council were hopping mad. Paul stopped dead. Now here was adventure, better than mucking about with David Monkton, who was rubbish at remembering Dan Dare stories. He waited while the fog swallowed up the boys' hoots and footsteps and the woman went inside. Assassin-like, he kept close to the fences till the pathway opened up on his left. The fog had sliced the top off the town's noise. Up the path he tiptoed, eased aside the flimsy boards and squeezed through.

It was colder, foggier than on the pathway and the street. Before his eyes things hardly moved at all. Newspaper, was that? A piece of tarpaulin from one of the barges? He stood transfixed by this seeing and not seeing, his mind folding into itself. The fog was unhappy because it had been called down in midsummer. Or the water was, because it couldn't drag along. Hence the sobbing. Rubbing his eyes, he stared through the chalky air. The sobbing was somewhere to his right and, as he moved, the fog seemed to pull itself aside as if it, too, couldn't bear the smell. The figure, small, looking down, far from the starlings of Newbold Brakes, the roar of Wilkinson Packings. No scarf, Paul saw: perhaps it was stuffed into his pockets with his gloves and balaclava, a whole new bunch of conkers, the kitchen sink. How else to explain how they bulged?

Ok, Pauly? sounded in his head. The small shoulders

heaved. Magic. The arms wrapped tight as if pleading for heat from this unforgiving day. Give you a game? John Muldoon would not forgive, or Christobel Foulkes. The new school year would not forgive, nor the mind-bending stretches of time ever after.

'Sometimes ya gotta do bad to do good.' The voice of Gabe Tomorrow, the Horizon King, rang through Paul's head as it had a few nights ago in the living room. His mother had paused in her hunt for thread and wrinkled her nose: 'Ya gotta? Can't they speak properly? And what sort of talk is that? Do bad to do good. If I tried it, Health Office'd have me out on my ear.'

Paul didn't know what Gabe meant and his words got no clearer as he moved forward, reached out a hand. The fog tightened again. Sounds warped out of true. 'Thought it was a neighbour's old toilet,' the woman in the house might have said after, if she'd heard. 'Like one of them jets, the flushes are. Mine's the same. Council keep promising to come round to fix them but…phuh, talk to yourself.'

Lychgate. Paul stroked the trellis's twining leaves, willing the feel of Mrs Middleton's magic tree back into his fingers. At the back of the classroom, the desk up against the wall. Under the lid, the scarf. Sometimes ya gotta. Good out of bad. By doing? Letting? Which, Gabe? Did I copy you right? But the credits had rolled and Mum had said, 'Right you lot, pyjama time.'

And now his mother stood at the other end of the trellis tunnel and his sisters' heads poked out from behind her. She spoke, he read her lips. What time do

106

you call this? Well? She shifted her weight. Maybe a change of tone. Paul…Paul?

Between him and her a window. So thick, so close that, as he opened his mouth, the pane fogged.

First published in *Theaker's Quarterly Fiction #59, Spring 2017*

Bugsy And Wally

I named them Bugsy and Wally, and they owed their life to a miracle. They lived beyond my uncle's farmhouse in Laurencetown, County Limerick. A tree-thickened drive swept round to a road gate that hadn't been opened for as long as anyone could remember. To the right was an embankment. If you scrambled up it and looked over, you saw slurry, a lake of grey-brown in the corner of the field my uncle rented from Willy McCarthy. Bugsy and Wally lurked there, keeping themselves tucked out of sight.

Or so it seemed to a seven-, eight-, nine-year-old with his head full of space travel and jungle adventures, the stuff of comics and films in the early Sixties. My home life was among flaring chimneys; the only acreage I knew was a wilderness of roofs. Summers at Laurencetown were something else. Every inch of the farm had a story to tell, and I set about telling them. Milk churns became toppling rocks in the Badlands. Uncle Mick's trap became a sky-chariot whose triumphs would shortly eclipse Sputnik, wipe the smile off Yuri Gagarin's face. Uncle Mick himself was either the Lone Ranger or Ming the Merciless, depending on his mood.

Inevitably, Bugsy and Wally stepped into my storybook. To any outsider, they'd have just been pink pigs. But that was where the miracle came in. Nobody knew about them, I was sure. They never ventured into Uncle Mick's farmyard. No one seemed to feed them, though they were hefty enough. Summer after summer, there they were, protected by their magical slurry.

Some instinct told me never to mention them to the adults. By that age, I knew the business of farms well enough, and I sensed that any betrayal of them would stop Uncle Mick in the middle of whatever he was doing: 'Jays, I clean forgot that pair,' I could hear him say, before rooting out his special knife, calling to one of the farm-boys that he had need of strong, steady hands. Besides, the grown-ups had their own fun. I heard it at night, smelt it curling under my bedroom door: smoke-language in the scent of Kensitas or the woefully mis-named Sweet Afton. Whisper-words from those who, in the day's hard sun, took on the world full-throatedly. Names from the land they unfolded like oilcloth and stepped into once I'd been bundled upstairs—names of gods, I guessed, so reverently did they handle them, my irreverent family. Hammarskjold. Rainier. DiMaggio, shadowed by a woman, possibly Marion or Marlene, usually defined as 'a glory girl'. Churchill—always a pause after that one. An Irish pause.

'One man in his time plays many parts,' says Shakespeare. Bugsy and Wally had one man, any man, entirely defeated. They were my sidekicks in Precinct 49. Together, we tracked down Scarface You-name-him and his hoods. Once the latest case was closed, we'd stand thoughtfully by the slurry, contemplating the streets of Everytown and our mission to make them safer for the honest folk. They were my boffins when we wrested the planet from mosquitoes big as blimps—my guides when we set out to find the Lost Valley of the Emperors, oddly disguised as McCarthy's stream.

This last was the pigs' finest hour. Noiselessly I

crossed the field's treacherous sands, past palms, through mirages. Not so noiselessly, Bugsy and Wally followed in a roundabout amble, their special tracking method. After many days, after battles with rabies, Yellow Jack, German measles, we found the Lost Valley, routed the evil spirits that had enslaved it and restored peace to the Emperors (all of whom were conveniently alive at the same time, which allowed my trackers and me a good old bask—'Gentlemen, don't mention it…hey, you take her easy…').

I should perhaps have lived out the rest of my life with the Emperors. Turning from the stream, I saw that the field was full of cows and horses. Had Bugsy and Wally's shenanigans drawn them in? Were they possessed by the Lost Valley's evil spirits (which now had to go wherever the work was)? The cows and horses circled, thundered. Shedding my explorer's mantle, I was again a nine-year-old boy, confused about which would be worse, mom's black-veil rhetoric or a doomsday turn from Uncle Mick. Ingloriously I shot through the chaos, diving into the embankment just as Uncle Mick strode through the gate and the air was filled with godlessness. I hid among the grasses, listening while, with cries of *Get out of all that!*, he emptied the field. At some point, Bugsy and Wally ambled back, unconcerned as ever. New York streets, blimpish mosquitoes, wreaking animal chaos—all the same to them. As Joe Friday from *Dragnet* had it, 'Just doing the job, ma'am.' I was dispatched to bed at an irrational hour; the smoke-words came curling early.

The following summer, there they were, gone. I tried mounting new space missions, taking on the streets of

Los Angeles. I even thought I'd drop in on the Lost Valley. But it wasn't the same. You can't hatch a plan or josh about with thin air. You can't save the world with ghosts.

First published in *Gold Dust, Issue 27——June 2015*

My Mother's Major

The sun channels across the tablecloth, flares and fades on the walls. On the mantelpiece, postcards flash back the light: a miniature Ullswater turns ocean-blue. The sun pokes about a pocket matador perched on a Majorcan ashtray; gives a lick of unearthly paint to the serving hatch. But soon all will darken, and it will be time to draw the curtains on the autumn day. Left edge over right, mother always insists: the other way creates ruckles, which means chaos.

I remember when dad sealed the serving hatch up. She remembers, too: wanted it kept open. They had words about it, drizzling over several days. Memories of dad are much with her, especially after the trip we've just made—clearing, replacing the water, lamenting the dilatory attitude of the groundsmen. The sun banks over the rooftops opposite. The roads will be choked now. I'll give it another hour. Besides, mother is disposed to talk.

'He knew that Major, your father. Right article he was. Never forget the way she looked at me. "What day is it, nurse? He'll ask." Poor creature.'

I've heard this one many times; I've heard them all. No matter. Time is ticking. It will vanish over the roofs with another sun on another day, taking with it this room, the postcards, the poised matador, the voice that speaks now. I relax in my chair. Mother's words turn the room back forty years. I see my satchel, scored with the names of midfielders, dumped under the serving hatch; and my school shoes, squashed at the heels, lying alongside it, when they should be in the hall cupboard, there being a place for everything. Mother's cream cardigan and brown slacks disappear; again she is in her ocean-blue—the colour of the Ullswater postcard—round white collar, watch over breast pocket, black felt hat with the badge on the side, a gentle indentation at the crown. An air-stewardess's, really: odd for a district nurse.

'I said to Miss Rennison, "I can't bear to go in any more." Not that I meant it. Who'd have looked after the old lady? Home helps just appeared once in a blue moon. None of the others would have them on their books. Just muggins here.'

The Crowleys. Mother and son. The Swinging Gate in Belville High Street. Free House. Flaking paint and plaster. Inside, a bar and a snug, brown as chestnuts from years of smoke and dust. Only the sign above the door was shiny: 'Major Alfred Crowley, licensed to sell intoxicating liquor…' 'That was a joke,' says mother. 'Most of it went down his own throat. Slewed at ten in the morning, I saw him, more than once. Him and his cronies, drinking the old lady's roof off her head after closing-time. I told your father not to go in there. Took no notice, of course.'

Major Crowley: first name, not achieved rank. Never anywhere near a gun, except if a fair pitched up between Wolverhampton and Dudley. But an uncle had done sterling work at Ypres, and his promotion was proudly enshrined through his nephew's christening. Stumpy man, Major: voice full of gravel, belt slung under his belly. Teddy Boy quiff, grey-black.

Rumours clung to him, principally that he ran cock-fights up on the Welsh border till the dad died and he

113

took over the pub. Better at that, it seemed, than at the publican's trade: abusive to customers, many of whom shifted ground to the newer pubs on nearby estates; abusive to dad, who he knew was married to 'that nuss'—but dad would buy a round and ignore him. Abusive most of all to Rene, his mother, whom he would clout regularly, thereby (it was reckoned) hastening the various conditions which required mother's attention.

Sometimes he would stun his patrons: stand at the foot of the oak stairs by the bar, holler way up to the top of the house. Sooner she was gone the better, he'd call. A leech on his profits. What kind of bleddy name was Major? Why hadn't they given him a proper name? Teased beyond endurance he'd been, all his life, and she bleddy knew it. Once the last punter was out and he'd slid the bolts on the night, the game went further. He'd creep up on her, tell her that next day, or the day after, he'd ask her a question. If she didn't answer straight off—and here, like a ten-pin bowler, he would swing his hand past her bowed head.

'She told me everything,' says mother, adjusting a leg of her slacks. 'Not as gone in the head as he thought. Daft questions, he came up with. Can't remember half of them.'

I can. What was the first car his dad drove? Who was the youngest of Salter Bros, Scrap Dealers, Darkhouse Lane? Did Auntie Beverley's Alec emigrate to South Africa and then New Zealand, or the other way round? How do you spell Ypres? Sometimes, as the old woman declined, Major would change tack. The questions

114

became simpler. He'd ask the same one twice running. What colour had her hair been? What was her maiden name? Her misting gaze would follow him when he came upstairs. She would try to guess the next question from his eyes.

'So this one day I was in there. Last call on the list. His majesty lets me in, then goes off down the cellar. And there she is, just a nightie on in that freezing, poky bedroom. Gripped my arm like a navvy, mind, frail as she was. "What day is it, nurse? He'll ask. He's made a big thing of looking at the calendar. He'll belt me if I don't know." Then I turn round and there he is. Gives us a royal mouthful, says he can do what he likes. Those as don't know the day of the week have no place under his roof. Orders me out, if you please, and her dressings half-done.'

The last straw: 'So off I trot to Rennison. She knew the score damn fine. Couldn't care less, though—with her smarmy smile, all that guff about old age, about romancing.' Well, she wouldn't. I'd heard her condemned often enough. Poacher turned gamekeeper. Indifferent nurse at best, but supervisor now, shoving the rest about, swanning around in a Ford Consul. 'Romancing my eye,' says mother. 'I studied Rene Crowley's hairline. I saw what I saw. Sly bugger, him.'

Sharp, my mother's eyes, even now. Able to pick out the keepsakes of violence under healthy heads of hair. As were Dr McGhee's. Inverness man, army doctor till long after the war. Miss Rennison's hero: well, he'd come bearing a petrol can once when she'd let her Consul run dry in Lower Gornal. He'd been rushing out of the

Health Office when he heard mother—'having a set-to with ladyship.' Mother wrinkles her nose. 'She gives him the eye. Madame du Barry. "That the Crowleys you're talking about?" says he. Rennison goes all purry, starts on about the mother, the delusions of the elderly. "I've heard enough about him," he says. "Locals give you the word, if nobody else does." And he stares hard at Rennison. Red as a cherry, her. "Right," says Dr, "both of you with me at Crowley's, ten o'clock tomorrow." Rennison starts blustering about some meeting. "Cancelled," says Dr. "Ten o'clock."'

Santiago is the capital of Chile. Mother learned that in school. She remembered it again next morning, when Dr McGhee hammered on the door of The Swinging Gate and Miss Rennison wondered aloud about decorum in doctor-patient relations, and a gravelly voice upstairs kept on and on, so that people halted on the street and called *Shame!* 'I'll give him the capital of Chile,' yelled Dr McGhee, hurling himself at the door. It gave: 'One bolt still on, mind,' says mother. 'But he bent it all to bits. McGhee for you. My champion.'

Halfway up the stairs, they heard the thud, then a whistle of breath, long and slow, as of a voice gathering itself for blasphemy. 'You're a disgrace to humanity, Crowley,' says mother now, quoting her champion warmly. But a woman's voice then, rising like a banshee's as they crowded into the poky room: 'Santiago! Santiago!' And Rene Crowley sinking to her knees over her son, and Dr McGhee cursing as he kneels on the other side, reaches over, parts her hair, sees the purple, the mottling. 'Santiago,' she repeated, as though the word were a gun

116

still smoking.

'That stroke was coming like Christmas,' says mother. 'All his drinking, guts like the side of a house. He went convalescent out Chapel Ash way. Never recovered. Waste of taxpayers' money. Even your father said that.'

And Rene, a new, somehow younger woman, sold up and moved to Much Wenlock, to be with Auntie Beverley. Alec, Beverley reminded her, moved to New Zealand first, then South Africa. But Rene realised she'd known that all along: told mother so when she phoned to thank her for all her kindness.

'Don't know where she got this number. Office wouldn't have let it out. I didn't care, though. Her voice was different when she rang. Easier. Almost posh. Mind, I think her family were a cut above. That probably got the son's goat as well. Thought he should have had his own box at the Wolves. 'Course, moment the new folk moved in your father stopped drinking there. Drama done, time to change ground. Him all over.' Her voice quivers a little. Once, 'him all over' was a war cry. Now it's a prayer, as if for the day the Majorcan ashtray was plonked unbudgeably on the mantel.

It's all but dark. I tell mother to stay put, switch on the lamp by the TV and make for the curtains: 'Left edge over right,' she instructs, as though a world in which such neatness is honoured is also, inevitably, a world in which big-belly sons hit the floorboards in poky rooms, and mothers shake off the terror of the years and ascend to Shropshire.

I pick up my car keys. 'Next Thursday, then,' I say.

Mother gets stiffly to her feet: 'I'll sort out another

vase,' she says. 'Narrow neck. Don't want all the slugs in Christendom sloshing about over him.'

Or Major's ghost, perhaps, drawn by the slimy pulsations of its kind.

First published in *The Interpreter's House—issue 17—June 2001*

The Man With The Double Watch

'So I'm afraid,' he said, 'we shan't be proceeding further at this time.'

I let my eyes lose focus. I used to do that as a kid, quite a lot. Bored in lessons, I'd make my book, the classroom, the teacher all go fuzzy. Images would turn vague, hang together for a moment, then break up. It was like mucking about with a Victorian stereoscope. It was oddly restful.

It was restful now, as he spoke on, thanking me for the opportunity, assuring me that my work had been thoroughly evaluated. His regret, he said, was deep. I looked past his shoulder. A salad cart stood between us and the bar. Couples and families were circling it, pondering, drawing each other's attention to this or that bowl, digging spoons in, changing their minds. As I stared, their bodies broke up. A green salad floated above and to the left of its receptacle. A man walked over to a couple. I blurred him. By the time he said, 'Was it Pernod and a pint of Exhibition?', he was a man and a half.

'I'm so sorry to have to leave you,' my companion said now, 'but I'd better get on—rush-hour traffic and all that.' He offered a wheeze with some laughter poking through. Awkward, a bit self-deprecating. Practised. I allowed myself one last minute of rest, blurring the watch he held pointedly to his face. Something inside it seemed to ripple and tug. It split apart, so that there were two of it on his elastic wrist. The circumferences were just touching. Rush-hour traffic, he'd said. At three in the afternoon. Perhaps he knew the area better than I did.

119

Perhaps it was busier than it looked.

My voice started up obligingly. I heard it thanking him, knocking out a formula, *for your time and trouble* and all that. He wished me well: 'Oh, and I'll leave this with you,' he added, placing a manila folder before me. At the top was the date on which I'd posted the folder to him. It was some time back now, suggesting that, as he said, the contents had been considered seriously. Or perhaps suggesting nothing. Perhaps they'd been gathered in a rush, unread, before he set out. It had just seemed like a good sign, the length of time he'd had it. You have to hang on to them. Good signs. I had an urge to look inside, to see if the pages were in the same un-thumbed order as when I'd inserted them. Instead, I just considered the date at the top, the diagonal bar I always put through my sevens.

Hands were shaken. Alone, I tried the trick of the eyes on the folder. It wouldn't budge. I tried again, puzzled, even a little afraid, like someone robbed of their party piece by a change of atmosphere. I don't know how long I kept trying, but I suddenly found myself looking up at a situation: me all alone at a table with a padded bench and three chairs, and a group of five standing over me, evidently trying some tricks of their own, willing me to melt out of all that comfy space.

In the car park, I walked up and down, smoking. I pondered the man with the double watch. 'We shan't be proceeding further at this time.' 'At this time' was a pleasant little gloss, a curlicue of no-hope trying to be hopeful. He'd used it a hundred times. His tongue was born to it. Perhaps he was off to use it again. I stared

120

down to the road, then at the roundabout beyond. The occasional car or van went by. There was all the space in the world for an easy drive. 'Rush-hour traffic,' he'd said, jigging his two smart watches under my nose.

At times like these, tiny things always stick. They swell, dwarfing all other memories. Pulling out of the car-park, I saw a sign telling me to have a safe journey. Opposite, a chained board said *No Exit*. I'll remember that, I thought. When I'm trying to rebuild life, stick all the pieces together again, that dozy tableau will be right at the front of my mind. When I'm trying to remember something crucial, something that might just save other skins, all I'll see are *Safe Journey—No Exit*. It's the kind of thing newspapers use as a filler, under headings like *Just Look At This!* or *Our Funny Old World*. Folk send them in, get paid for them: ten quid, twenty, more. Perhaps I should come back and take a snap of them. It'd be a start, ten or twenty quid, since the unblurrable folder can't be taken any further. At this time.

As I drove along the dual carriageway, they all settled around me. Moon faces, hopeful faces. The faces of home. I saw them doing what they do: sliding clean dishes under counters, pinning earphones into place, fighting over the TV remote. But they'd be waiting, bound together more surely than in any mantelpiece photo:

'Am I looking at a winner?' I heard her say. 'So when does it all start?'

I saw the boy staring at me, gawky in his tee-shirt: *Alabama State Line,* it said, black letters on cherry-red. He didn't know what to do with his hand. It curled towards a thumbs-up, then went slack. A nod of expectancy troubled his impossible hair. He wanted me to spill the beans, so that he could mumble, 'Wow, fantastic.'

And now a ballet bag shoved him aside, and there was the princess. I imagined her jumping up and down. '*Yay! Yay!*' she yelled, pigtails flying.

A man's voice spoke of trust and cashed policies. 'I believe in you, brother of mine,' he said. 'That's why I pinned my shirt to your back.'

I saw myself at the lounge door, swaying a little. I spoke aloud. The car's interior made my small voice smaller. I told the waiting faces that there had been deep regret but also gratitude at the chance to evaluate the folder with a date at the top. 'I don't know why I do that,' I burbled. 'Put a diagonal bar across my sevens.'

With that, everything began to vanish. I saw my family miming in unfurnished space. Non-dishes slid behind invisible wood. The battle for the remote was just a dance of empty fingers. The mime got slower. Even their clothes began to disappear. They seized up. Lifting a hand from the wheel, I imagined touching each of them in turn. Hard. Cold.

I was scared of what lay ahead. Tired, too. My mind turned, hid itself back at the beginning. Again I felt her squeeze of my arm. That had started it all—or rather, ended the indecision, the months of talk.

It was a dreadful morning: pools in the lawn, draggled cats. Briefcase and bags were weighing down my left hand. I'd just realized that my keys were in my left pocket and was preparing to transfer the ballast when I felt it. A girlish squeeze, full of the old times. You'd think we were getting ready to walk out—to a pub's tatty welcome, then a dance, then the curious intimacy of a street lamp.

'You've convinced me,' she said. 'Go for it. Cautious-bones,' she added, her words smiling at the man she'd known for years, right up to that moment when I fished out my keys and a cat slithered past, blotching my trousers.

The day had changed as I drove off. The rain fell on everyone but me. Pedestrians were just too slow to miss tyre-loving puddles. Above the crowds, umbrellas fought, some flipping into bowls on sticks. But I walked from the car with a glowing shield about me. I could have been in an advert for pain relief.

A little while later, McDowell stared at me from the far side of a desk landscaped with pictures and a Newton's cradle, its balls arrayed shinily. His phone rang. Shooing off the caller, he pushed it away from him and resumed his stare.

'Heavens, you do surprise me,' he said. 'I thought you'd be with us for the duration.' A sigh escaped his lips, along with a word or two I didn't catch. Cautious-bones, perhaps. 'Might I ask about this…what do we call it? Venture? Leap in the dark?' He made the sound of an old man shaken from sleep. I'd never known him get any nearer than that to a laugh. Year after year, it had puzzled special guests at the Christmas socials—even frightened a few, who feared a doctor would be required. Blurring the cradle, I started to explain. The row of balls obliged my eyes by doubling in number. My stare spread them wide apart, then drew them together, overlapping them, making them kiss. By the time I'd finished, they were a silvery mush.

A sharp rattle brought me back to the now. It was raining hard. The hand that had imagined the cold feel of those dearest to me now flipped on the wipers. I thought of bad omens. How you don't have to look far to find them. How you create them yourself if you're not careful. That's how all those extravagant dinners made me feel now. They started a day or so after my words with McDowell. Celebrating the future, that's what they were about. Marking my transformation from Cautious-bones to a gutsy leaper in the dark.

I went along with it all, though I should have seen that it was unwise, a delirious counting of chickens. I couldn't remember much about them now. The restaurants and pubs melded into each other. This waitress's name was Karen; that sweet counter offered lovely profiteroles. Only one time stood out, thanks to a misunderstanding. Suddenly a huge cake was plonked down before me and the entire room launched into *Happy Birthday*.

'But it is your birthday,' my brother said, putting his arm round my shoulder, holding hard. 'Your rebirth-day.' He repeated the phrase all evening, each time a little more hiccupy than the last.

My brother. The chief investor in my leap in the dark. The one who'd always had me down as the lucky lad, always rolled his eyes at my inability to see it. Perverse, he called me.

I thought of the evidence he'd trotted out over the years. A winning ticket in a school raffle, which I'd lost, found, accidentally surrendered to the washing machine in a jeans pocket and finally grabbed as it fluttered above the clothesline. A Christmas when dad had squared it with a pub landlord so that we could accompany him, and a jukebox started playing Elvis Presley's *Follow That Dream* just as I walked past. Girls who, my brother insisted, sighed and pined for me, though I never discovered who they were.

There were other miracles, too, as flimsy as these. He'd turned them all into articles of faith. 'High time you followed that dream,' he said after one of those dinners, reminding me that he'd seen to his final policy and the money would be in my account soon, ready for the gilded future. He'd have had a thing or two to say to the man with the double watch. I wondered what he'd say to me. I imagined him standing there, *Follow That Dream* on his lips. The words broke down into a quavery hum. His mouth hung open, silent.

The motorway was in sight. More signs, no doubt, winking at me through the worsening rain. *Spray. Slow Down. Caution.* I thought of the folder, how my eyes had failed to budge it. Again I felt afraid. Surely I hadn't lost the trick. It was so relaxing, such a haven. Surely I hadn't lost it. I got myself comfortable. My fingers eased their pressure on the wheel—almost slid off. '*Safe journey,*' said that sign in my head. '*No Exit,*' goofed its sidekick. A tide of cars and heavy rigs gathered from the right. I hadn't lost the trick. Surely.

First published in *Muscadine Lines: A Southern Journal—November-December 2008*

Danny, George And The Frogs Of Evening

'And stop gawping at them.' Stephanie didn't speak unkindly. She looked at them too, when occasion and angle of vision allowed. But this evening it was Neil's chance again. He had the chair facing into the dining room. A right pig's ear he was making of it, too: leaning forward, tilting his head. So obvious. Stephanie just had to intervene. If they gawped back, he wouldn't care, but she'd die a thousand deaths.

Neil's fork stirred automatically, pushing his tagliatelle to the edge of his plate. He could have been a school kid faffing with mashed potato. He didn't look back at Stephanie:

'They won't notice,' he said. 'They can't see anyone else in this room.'

'Neil!'

'Oh, all right.' His fork urged the tagliatelle back to the centre of the plate. He loaded up a mouthful. But now Stephanie couldn't help herself. Old ways are best ways, she thought, and dropped her napkin by her foot. Leaning to retrieve it, she turned for a quick gawp herself.

They always sat in the same chairs: the blonde on the left, the raven-haired one on the right. As usual, they were tilted towards each other, the back legs of their chairs off the ground. They looked like gilded bookends about to collapse on each other. Their whispers carried, edgy and quick, amid the roomful of talk and working cutlery. Stephanie's French was patchy at best. Neil could

126

have told a Frenchman that the cap of his cousin was on the peg of his auntie but had never found occasion to do so. Still, they guessed the unvarying cause of the whispers. It lay under the table between the women's restless feet: a black Labrador with sad eyes, now pushed shut by the lie of its forepaws.

'Parisian women always look so elegant,' murmured Stephanie.

Neil shook his head at his rapidly-clearing plate: 'Here we go again. Look, how do you know they're from Paris?'

'Oh, they must be.'

'Anyone can get that look these days,' said Neil. 'Chain stores and that. Look at your Gemma, how she dolls herself up. She's hardly set foot out of Staffordshire.'

Stephanie reflected on her sister, glamorous yet rooted firmly at home. She conceded—to herself, anyway—that her assumption about the women was clichéd. She didn't like that side of her nature. Neil was the same, despite the 'been there, done that' routines he occasionally went in for. Both of them knew that their horizons could stand some broadening. That was partly why they'd ventured to Tuscany for an April break.

Three days earlier, they'd walked round the dining room when it was empty. Somewhere over their heads, their room was being readied. Near an open window, their hire car was still cooling down, its bodywork ticking.

'Look about,' the receptionist had kindly urged. 'I call you when your room is done.'

They could have been potential buyers, peering at the fitments, the paintings on the wall. Now they met between two tables, now they wandered apart.

'"*La Rizinia*",' Neil had whispered to himself, wondering how you savoured a foreign name.

Stephanie had murmured 'San Gimignano,' baffled by a detail in the hotel's literature. *An easy two kilometres' stroll from us to San G,* it had chummily promised. But they'd just driven past the town. It was a sight further than that. And she'd been looking forward to an easy stroll.

'Zuzuzu.' The unintelligible word had brought them together at one of the terrace windows, frowning at each other, craning their necks. From a different direction came 'Tatata.' Then they'd spotted the silver car. Beside it, two women were towering over a Labrador. One, blonde, repeated 'Zuzuzu.' The dog shuffled round, pressing its head against her leg. The other, hair black as night, tried 'Tatata' again, peevishly this time. The dog stayed put for a moment. Then it got itself upright with some difficulty, wheeled about and fell against the other pair of legs.

'Ha!' said Raven-hair, at which Blonde, now peeved herself, shoved the car's hatchback open. In went the dog, and they left.

Neil and Stephanie exchanged perplexed looks. 'Zuzuzu?' said Neil, his lip curling. But then the receptionist was at their side, nodding from one to the other with pretty affability. They went up to their room.

That evening, they'd found themselves at the next-but-one table to the women. The women's tics and mannerisms were subtly hypnotic. Stephanie, who had the better view, found herself watching the back legs of their chairs, the way they rose and fell as if obeying the ebb and flow of the women's whispers. Mainly they were off the floor, so intense was the exchange. To judge from the downward-pointing fingers, the way one or the other woman suddenly ducked to look under the table, its focus was the Labrador. Flopped out between their agitated feet, it looked as though it wished it were anywhere but there. Neil concurred with its wish in his own way.

'Bit much, letting a dog loll about where folk are eating.' He looked sharply at Stephanie. 'You're going to say it's OK, aren't you? You're going to say *When in Rome.*'

Stephanie wasn't going to say anything. She felt sorry for the dog—and for the slingbacks that Blonde was wearing, which were getting some mean treatment from her twisting, stubbing feet.

The next night, they'd been seated three tables away. Still, Neil had a half-decent view.

'Raven's doing some serious hair-twisting,' he said. As best she could, Stephanie had looked round—just in time to see Blonde shoot to her feet, urge the dog from under the table and steer it out of the dining room. Raven chuckled to herself and disposed of some morsel caught on her lower lip. Then, gingerly, she lowered the back legs of her chair and stared blankly towards the evening sun. A moment later, Blonde reappeared at the dining room door. Up went Raven's chair-legs again. Blonde walked to the table slowly, draggingly, like a petulant child who needs wooing back to compliance. Raven wasn't having any of it. She continued to stare ahead. Again Blonde withdrew.

Now, tonight, as the women hissed and the dog tried

to hide under its paws, Stephanie realised that she and Neil had let two full days of their break slip clean away. They'd explored the little villages around '*La Rizinia,*' got lost amid San Gimignano's squares and ramparts. They had visited Volterra, where Stephanie had bought a pot which, in Neil's view, wouldn't stand the journey home. 'Look,' he'd said. 'Cracking already.' But the women and their dog were forever with them, three shadows across every view.

Endlessly they speculated: about the women's relationship, who owned the dog, why they were apparently battling over it, whether they'd bribed the hotel so the dog would never leave their sight. As Neil ruefully said, they could have saved the holiday money, sat in some random café and made up stories about the first customers they saw.

In Volterra, on the second day, they'd seen them for real. Blonde was outside a *parfumerie,* triumphant above the Labrador. Raven was inside, trying to look interested in the wares but shooting troubled glances at her companion and their mutual charge.

'Hello.' Stephanie had spoken impulsively, leaving Neil's hiss of 'Look, don't bother them' hanging in the air, tardy and ungallant. 'You're at "*La Rizinia*"'; then, backtracking helplessly, '"*La Rizinia*"—vous—moi aussi.'

Blonde gave a pert shrug, as if to say, yes, people stay in hotels. Instantly, Raven was by her side, looking from Blonde to Stephanie and Neil. She frowned inquisitively at Blonde and rubbed her thumb along her finger. Blonde shook her head furiously.

'Stroll on,' Neil had said as he and Stephanie retreated.

'Raven thought we were trying to pay for her pal's attentions.'

'She thought something,' said Stephanie, taking a last look back. From between the women's legs, the dog seemed to regard her with tragic eyes.

'OK.' Neil dispatched the last strand of tagliatelle and laid his cutlery crosswise on his plate, the way that made Stephanie despair. 'Dessert? Cheese and stuff?'

Stephanie shook her head. The women were nowhere near the end of their meal. Their whispers were giving her a headache. Walking past reception, they spotted a brochure for all kinds of entertainment in San Gimignano next day. Picking it up, Neil smiled at the receptionist and waved it:

'What's going on tomorrow?' he asked. The receptionist explained that tomorrow was Liberation Day.

'Ah.' Neil's nod was all-knowing. 'When Mussolini got the shove.'

Perplexed, the receptionist made a little pushing motion to herself, trying to see Il Duce's fate in terms of a jostle in the street. Stephanie rescued the pair of them.

'Is it worth going?'

'Oh, yes—bands, exhibitions.' The receptionist looked grave. 'Our history,' she confided.

Stephanie smiled her thanks and drew her husband away. 'Got the shove,' she muttered as they toiled up to their room. 'Honestly, Neil.'

He was the first thing to catch their eye the next day: roly-poly, stubbled, his tie askew. A drum rose and fell against his stomach. He stood a little apart from the rest of the band, who in comparison were smartly turned out and a good deal taller than him. Neil closed his eyes and began tarrump-a-dumping along with the march. Stephanie kept hers open, roving the generous square in which San Gimignano's citizens mingled with visitors. Clothes of stylish cut brushed past knapsacks. Ice-cream and pizza carts traded mightily.

She felt an elbow in her ribs. Neil was watching the drummer again.

'Danny de Vito's in trouble,' he said.

For a second, Stephanie thought he'd miraculously translated a headline at a news stand. Funny thing to have as a lead story. Then again, it was an Italian name and they were doubtless proud to claim a Hollywood star as their own, whatever he'd done.

'Him,' Neil elaborated, gesturing at the drummer.

It was a matter of wonder that he could keep the beat. Everything apart from his hands was twisting and craning about.

'He's like a chicken on hot coals. Must have creditors on his tail,' said Neil. 'The Mob.'

Don't do a Godfather accent, prayed Stephanie. Mercifully, Neil didn't. Instead, he looked at the Liberation Day brochure and his watch: 'That memorial procession's starting in ten minutes,' he said. 'Should we make our way—?'

Stephanie shushed him: 'Look,' she said. Danny the drummer was now even further from the band. Half-turned from the crowd, he was peering at an alley off the square. Suddenly the drum was ditched and he was waddling off. His fellow musicians didn't bat an eyelid. At the entrance to the alley he jiggled a hand as if in greeting. He all but disappeared. Only the back of his ruinous jacket was visible, shifting from side to side.

'He's having a dance,' laughed Neil. 'Or some thug's got him by the collar. Told you—creditors. Let's have a shufti.'

Leaving the crowd, they got as near to the alley as prudence allowed. Suddenly, Danny came dancing backwards. There was Blonde bearing down on him, making 'hurry, hurry' gestures. Their hands blurred together. A wad of notes, tidy enough from where Neil and Stephanie were standing, shot from her hand through his and into the unspeakable jacket. Both of them retreated up the alley. A moment later, the Labrador emerged, shaking, bewilderment in its eyes. As if in a cartoon, Danny's arm shot out of the alley, grabbed the scruff of its neck and hauled it away.

Neil and Stephanie stood frozen. Then, 'Come on,' he said and steered her right to the mouth of the alley. As they reached it, they almost collided with Danny. A transformation had occurred, as though the possession of so much money had automatically smartened him up. With a bright grin and a spring in his step, he sauntered back to his band, picking up the beat as though he'd never left. He'd even found time to straighten his tie.

That evening, Raven's feet were still beneath the table. Blonde's locked this way and that, as though she were practising an elaborate box-step.

She was the picture of distress.

'What's she doing?' muttered Neil, who had

reluctantly conceded that Stephanie was a more discreet watcher and granted her the better view.

'Flapping her hands. She keeps…hang on…' Casually, Stephanie turned her head a little, resting it on her hand. 'She keeps saying the same thing. Go? Yes, go. The dog just go.'

'She's spinning Raven a line.' It was a line that had been bought by everyone else at '*La Rizinia*'. As she performed, Blonde got sympathetic smiles from the other tables. Patrons exchanged glances, shaking their heads sadly. Only Raven remained impassive.

'Have you finished?' asked Neil.

Stephanie pushed her plate aside.

As they left the dining room, they saw the receptionist talking to an American couple who'd just checked in that evening. She gestured towards the diners.

'And he just disappeared?' asked the man. 'Jeez, that's too bad.'

'We have a Labrador,' said the woman. 'I'd go crazy if anything happened to Genghis.'

Neil's arm was seriously squeezed. 'We've got to tell someone,' hissed Stephanie.

'To the terrace, I think.' Neil spoke with blokeish pleasure, as though she weren't there.

When they were on the terrace, and he was eyeing his untouched lager, she said, 'I know we're on holiday. I know you and your "don't get involved" routine. Creeping after Danny in that square—no more than a giggle to you. But Neil—the dog didn't just vanish.'

'Be a pile of kebabs by now.'

'Oh, don't be disgusting. Look, are you going to drink

that? And why did you buy me this?' She nodded at an indeterminate fruit drink.

'Play the game, Steph,' said Neil. 'We're a couple of tourists in a world of their own, taking in the evening.' He leaned forward: 'You think I don't get involved?' As he spoke, the women emerged and headed down the drive to the gates. Blonde was still shaking. Raven held her by the arm as a solicitous friend might hold a widow.

'Bingo,' said Neil. 'My prayer's been answered. Come on.'

The women turned left. The road descended gently to a bend. Neil walked behind them, not too close, keeping to the verge to muffle his footsteps. Behind him, Stephanie was fretful, a little afraid: 'Not like this, Neil. I said, tell someone—the receptionist or—'

Neil stopped and held up a hand. The women reached the bend and disappeared left onto a path. He turned: 'I'll go alone if you like.'

For a moment, they stood staring at each other, their breaths falling in and out of sync. A new sound announced itself. At first it sounded like tiny handsaws cutting into wet wood. Then it became a chorus of frogs, a thick, wide blanket of sound from the direction the women had taken. Stephanie gave an acquiescent sigh:

'But we should still tell someone,' she repeated.

The path from the bend led through a marshy meadow. Pools abounded, thatched over with tall reeds. Off to the right was an open lake, ringed by the frogs' insistent singing.

Stephanie pulled abreast of Neil. The women were some way ahead. In the gathering dusk, they could see

Blonde trying to tug her arm free from Raven. At first she tried modestly, but then her gestures became more extravagant. Over the frog-chorus she whimpered, then yelped. Raven clung on.

'Watch where you're treading,' said Neil. 'Cracking twigs and that.'

Suddenly Stephanie clapped her hand over her mouth.

'What? You going to be sick?'

She nodded frantically ahead. Another figure had risen out of the marshy verge and was waiting for the women. Neil squinted: 'Stroll on—it's Danny.'

After her shock, Stephanie felt strangely relieved. What matter that she was no linguist? Part of her was convinced that they were about to witness a scene in which some silly misunderstanding was cleared up. The dog would be produced. Blonde would explain all to Raven, who would stay silent a moment, then throw her head back and laugh. The trio would walk back towards them, allowing her to try out 'Good evening…what a pleasant day it's been'—in French and Italian. The Labrador would snuffle at Neil's feet. He would find a hunk of wood and throw it an impossible distance, overdoing things as usual.

She was so caught up in this fancy that it took a dig in the ribs from Neil to make her really look. Facing in their direction, Blonde was on her knees. Danny stood behind her, one hand pressing down on her shoulder, the other pinning her head to his belly. They could only see Raven's back. Her legs were splayed, her hands locked behind her neck. She was control, triumph. On the lake, the frogs doubled their song. They could have been a

Colosseum crowd straining for a gladiatorial kill. It was a miracle that Blonde's cries outdid them.

And now a fourth figure emerged from way down the path: immaculately coiffed and suited, moving with the ease of an early-morning walker—a sleek bugger, in Neil's estimation.

'He looks like George Clooney,' breathed Stephanie, her anxiety yielding to different emotions. 'God.'

George gave Danny's shoulder a fraternal pat, regarded Blonde for a moment, then walked round to Raven. Their embrace was passionate. Blonde's cries turned to whimpers and sank below the frogs' uproar.

'Neil, they'll see us!'

'Here,' whispered Neil, hustling her back a few yards to the overhang of a tree. 'Go on, round, round.'

The refuge of the leaves emboldened him. He goggled through the branches like a boy at his first film. Out on the path, the quartet were still. George had released Raven and was now hunkered down by Blonde. Her head hung forward. He tousled her hair like a methodical sadist. Danny opened his mouth—for an oath, perhaps, or a chuckle. The frogs were delirious.

Neil nudged Stephanie's arm:

'I've got it,' he whispered. 'George is Raven's hubby. The dog was—is—theirs. Blonde's her loony friend or weird sister or something.' Stephanie stared at him in amazement. He could have been tackling a three-part question in a pub quiz.

He rolled on: 'The women came here to sort something out—some aggro, a personal thing. It didn't go Blondie's way, so she saw to the dog—or thought she

137

did. God knows how she hooked up with Danny. Anyway, he double-crossed her. And now, here's George to…you know, round things off.'

Stephanie grimaced at him: 'So where's the dog? And what happens now?'

They could hardly have guessed. Blonde started up again. This time her cry was long, unwavering. It was a tide on which the frogs fanned out their voices, soprano to bass. Up and up it rose till she threw back her head, grinning at Raven through her noise. Danny pulled her to her feet, while George stepped behind Raven and sent her sprawling. They could have been telepathic Punch-and-Judy men. Behind the tree, Stephanie and Neil squeezed the life out of each other. George stood over Raven and reached inside his jacket. From somewhere in the dusk came the last glint of pure sun. It lit his withdrawing hand—his watch strap; a ring; something as sleek as he was, as black as her hair. The frogs sang on, their voices making momentary space for a new sound, hot and quick.

Neil was too late finding Stephanie's mouth. Her scream drew footsteps down the path. 'I love you,' cried Neil. Hands pulled back branches, something black and lumbering made straight at Neil, Stephanie felt fingers pressing, locking.

At that moment, back at the hotel, a waiter passed by the empty terrace and noticed the two untouched drinks. He took up the lager, sipped, decided it wasn't completely flat and had a swig.

The receptionist came out. Catching him, she wagged

a playful finger, at which he proffered the fruit juice like a bouquet. She took it and he toasted her, his words knowing and elaborate. About to sip, she paused and cocked an ear, frowning. He looked quizzically at her. For a moment they were absolutely still. Then she shrugged. They clinked glasses.

First published in *Etchings 5, 'The History Of...' issue, 2008*

The Summer He Slipped Away

Written politely, left where it could be seen. The door closing soundlessly. The lane, the turn, the top of the main street. Cold for July, even that early. Just a lorry on the way to the creamery and one man unlocking a shop way down the other end. Then the promising sound of an engine. A hopeful thumb out.

'Limerick?' asked Richard.

'Ah,' said the van driver, 'I'm for Athlone. I could drop ye at Thurles, you'd easy cut across from there.'

'Remind me again how your little rhymes go.'

''There's Geoff Hurst…that's a first…'

An impatient sigh: 'Never rated him. He'd've been nothing without the others in '66.'

'A Doo Ron Ron…a two-one. My mate Jim Laycock coined that. He—'

'What a clever lad. And?'

'A Desmond…Desmond Tutu—'

'—that blackie troublemaker they've started on about—?'

'—for a 2:2…a Thora Hird…third…and a Pass.'

'Like foot of the class.'

'Yes. No honours. An ordinary degree. You don't get—'

'Well, you dodged that at least. So…what can you do,' Richard's father adds, looking around what he alone calls his workshop, 'with a Desmond? Or in a tutu?'

Sod, thinks Richard, I handed you that on a plate. A gentleman's degree, Jim Laycock had called it in the

140

Union bar after the last exam. And you could imagine the Scarlet Pimpernel with a 2:2 or even Bertie Wooster if Jeeves had found a devilish way to feed him answers on the quiet. *Might I suggest, sir…ahem… Jeeves, you're a wonder!* Dave Prince was well-oiled, circuiting the Union bar: 'End of an era, eh? End of an era!' Those big unfocused eyes.

Richard smiles at the memories. Tightens his lips. What can I do, Dad? I don't want to do a thing.

'Mum says to bring in the bookends you were doing.'

A glance around the extension-room filled plausibly with cuts of wood, saws and a vice still shiny. Bookends? No sign of anything like. No disturbance of the dust that was massing nicely the last time Richard looked in, at Easter. Your unstoppable optimism again, Mum. Or you asked me to ask because you're tired of getting your head bitten off.

'They'll be in when they're in.' Dad's twitch. 'Things take the time they take. I keep telling her that. So…something like teaching?' A quiet snort, disbelief refined with the years. 'Want to start now? Teach me?' He picks up a plane, runs a finger up and down the end: 'Please, sir, what's the proper name for this?'

The door sticks as Richard tries to close it.

'Have to lift it up with the handle,' calls Dad. 'Keep telling you that. Remind me,' he adds through the time-chamfered wood, 'what degrees did your sisters get? Hursts, weren't they?'

That summer. Unemployment on the up along with rubbish in the charts, save for 10cc. Decent, 'I'm Not In

Love'. But everything else was stalling. For now, though, just tonight's meal to get through, then off down to uni again, with friends till the proper end of term. Squeeze, Richard told himself, squeeze every drop from those days. I should have waited till afterwards to tell him what I got. What is it with these impulses? Folk-conditioning, Dave Prince would call it in his rare sober moments, him and his anthropologicals. A spur in the blood.

That's what had made Richard sign up to what was probably the very last family holiday, three weeks' time. No, never mind folk-conditioning: pragmatism, more like. Eke out the remains of the study grant with mum and dad paying the rest. Not that there'd be much for anyone to pay. Aunt Josie's cottage at their disposal, cousin Nora just up the way. A fortnight of all those voices—'So, the John Bulls are back in the Emerald Isle…'

Both sisters going: the Hursts. Both freeloading, with far less call than he had. They were raking it in: civil service, hospital consultancy. Shame Glenys's John couldn't make it. He didn't give a stuff: sang *Rule Britannia* just to get the rellies' goat. But the car market was doing fine—a miracle something was—so he was needed at the showroom. Have to get a few pub nights in with John, he thought, before I go: stock up on fortitude to take across the sea…or home again, as mum routinely said, even sang, when such a trip was in the offing. Well, she would. Home again, Kathleen. Jiggedy-jig.

When had he last seen the two Hursts? Whenever it was, their old attitude was undimmed: 'Still reading the paperbacks, Richard?' Glenys had asked him, Christmas, Easter, whenever. 'One fine day, some high-up will say those subjects are worthless. Your best bet, mate, a conversion course. Law, eh, Richard? Surely to God someone in those little stories makes like a lawyer. Copy them.' Some other time, Veronica had banged on about Erich von Däniken: 'Know it, Richard? *Chariots of the Gods?* That's one good read, sonny-boy. And no more far-fetched than the stuff you stick your nose in. Hamlet, Heathcliff…Christ.' A wrinkle of the nose and, of course, a giggle.

Honorary colleens, Glenys and Veronica, like dad was an honorary Pat. 'And here's our Richard, everyone. These days he's wearing a tutu.' He could imagine any of the three of them barking that in Aunt Josie's front room. Loud laughter, especially from Cahal, one of the Kilkenny crowd, Aunt Josie's favourite. Mum said he'd just landed a big meats job in the Garda. Loved needling, Cahal. Loved it too much some years back: Richard had beaten him senseless and was in heavy-rhetoric disgrace for the rest of the holiday. But now a policeman? The republic must be desperate, lads.

Swansea Port and fretting over customs and were they in the right lane. Glenys polishing bits of her new Austin Allegro during the wait, so dad following suit with his not-new Hillman Minx. Ah, but the boat. A great mansion—greater now it was passengers only, not stuffed with cattle below decks like they used to be when Richard was a kid. Plenty of places to be where the rest weren't.

Nice to grab that coffee with Mum, though. Really nice, too, those girls from Leicester he got talking to. Going over for work, hotels, Killarney. Now, that was something. A bellhop, he could be, Killarney too, or Dublin. Just his luck, of course, if Cahal pitched up at his particular hotel for some police junket. Worth the risk, though, and he'd be paid for hearing 'Hey you' and 'C'mere' in voices a cut above dad's. Get in with American tourists, maybe, play the English card, posh things up a bit...possibilities in New York, Philadelphia, Los Angeles. No...no, who says that? LA...

...and then the arrival announcement and Cobh going past and everyone pushing down to the sweltering car-decks and 'Drive On The Left' signs and Cork City, New Twopothouse, Charleville, Ardpatrick, Ballyroe, Aunt J's, hugs and 'Come you ins' and the 'tutu' joke— 'Good one, that. Ah now, wait till the rest hear'—and dad's finger-snap saying, damn it, Veronica, you got in first. And the big news about Pauline.

From Des Moines, Pauline, but not. Aunt Josie's daughter as everyone knew but no-one said. Sent off to be a nun, the shame of others packed in her suitcase. Not due to visit for another year, but there'd been a switch and now here she was, almost, five days' time. Accommodation needed rearranging but not to worry: the Horsfords down the lane were off visiting a daughter in New Zealand in a day or so and would be absolutely bloody well delighted if one of the arrivals house-sat. Or more than one?

'Well, now...': Glenys and Veronica conferring,

claiming the Horsford house, their deliberations eliciting 'Good girls' from dad and Aunt J and Uncle Francis, Aunt J's eldest brother, parked exactly where Richard had seen him whenever last time was, tilted at the fire, gobbing into the turf, Nosferatu hands.

'It's ok…I know the place.' Holdall scooped up, door opened, front gate squealing like last time. Hinge-oil like dad's bookends—pending, taking the time it takes.

'Hey, Richard we'll all be fine here till Pauline arrives. Then it's Vron and me down there, you're to go to Nora's.'

'God help her'—Dad, trying to make a love-the-stuff face at the glass of Powers.

'You'll just mess their house up. Richard!'

Richard walked down the crown of the lane. Mrs Horsford was at the gate of the pin-neat house with the lovely ship's-bridge front windows.

'Richie! Tired of all the chat already?'

'Sorry, I know you're not going till—'

'Never mind that. There's just me and Himself rattling round in here. Ah, welcome, welcome.' She smiled. Meant it.

Various trips before Pauline. The Wolfe Tones playing at Bulgaden Castle:

'Now, boys and girls, before the next song'—a wink—'who's in tonight from England?'

Sssssss from around the room.

'Jays, not us.' Dad slurringly stage-Oirish, rocking in his chair. Glynis's bleat, Veronica's giggles. The Sisters Ni Houlihan.

145

But Youghal was glorious and Richard swam out further than he'd ever done before. Racing the waves back, he trod water till he could make out the particular horseshoe of deckchairs and rugs, then swam out again.

'Man alive,' said Cousin Nora's Sean, 'you're not going back in my car, you're smelling of shite.'

'Oh God, Sean, why did I marry you?'

'Because you think I'm a dote, Nora, and I look like Redford.'

Glenys smoothed her rug: 'John sends his love to everyone, by the way.'

'So them harpies at the Post Office put you through to him?'

'At the price of ear-wigging.'

'Ah, Glen, they're devils that way.'

'He had a message for you, Richard. Can't remember it now. It'd help if you were around in the day. I'll bet you are mucking up the Horsford place.'

'We'd better come and check.' Veronica got herself comfier, a touch more pert-missy.

'I'd say Richie's already found the girl friend.' Sean's elbow made Richard jump.

'Or a dirty magazine,' said dad, staring up and shielding his eyes.

'Cyril,' hissed Mum, 'don't.' At dad's feet, Veronica giggled.

'Come on, sonny-boy, dry yourself off and get back in that tutu.'

Richard smiled.

'Don't, love,' Mum's eyes pleaded up at him.

Reaching down, Richard flicked dad's hand away: 'Of

course, darling. Help me with it, will you? You know I love all those little things.'

Dad got up to him and was smartly got down again. Shock, silence. On the way back, Richard was in Sean's car after all.

'Jesus Christ, Richie, your own father. What next? A Rumble in the Jungle?'

A slow walk up from the Horsfords' the following evening. Aunt J's front yard full. Cahal in the middle of a group, one hand pocketed, the other round a short: 'So I says, if you think Mr Conor Cruise O'Brien has a feckin' clue…' Uncle Seamus's crew from Emly, Uncle Martin's from Ardpatrick. Richard used to think Pauline was an Emly, his sisters that she was an Ardpatrick, but at some point Mum's murmuring put them straight.

Cahal. Richard's hand itches or maybe that's from yesterday. Flabby, dad's face, like his words. Twenty steps to the gate, nineteen, eighteen. Why was he bothering? Even among a houseful, his lot would still call up the old long-practised silence…save Mum, who'd try and have a grieving word.

A black figure flowing into the road before him:

'Ah, Richie. Look at the man you are.'

'Hey…hey, hello…'

What did you do with a nun? Handshake? Hug? Use her imposed name? Sister Mona Assumpta. Like someone out of Sly and the Family Stone. He just looked at her. Not anyone's daughter now, Pauline. Aunt Josie had unseen hands holding her in proper place. The district was willing to be tolerant: Pauline back for visits,

147

all the family round. And a nun—almost showbiz, that. Aunt Josie knew her part. A few words in quiet, maybe an afternoon out shopping together, public places, that was alright, like. And Josie, ah now, she was a mannerly lady. She'd never bid for a second to be the mother she was.

'Will we walk?' said Pauline. 'Inside's like Rome when they smoke out a new Pope.'

'Should you be saying that? Shouldn't you—?'

'The town way?'

Horsfords' drifted by on their right:

'They have that place done up grand, I'd say'—a coy nudge—'your place of exile.'

'So…how's Des Moines? Idaho, yes? One of the "I" states?'

'Iowa, Richie, and it is what it is.' She stopped, looked him up and down. 'Last time I saw you, you'd have been sixteen. Just done your…certificates?'

'O-levels.'

'Yes. God forgive me, I remember your father giving out about how you weren't able for them. Just like he's giving out now, above. Desmond Tutu.' She wrinkled her nose. 'What an awful word to use about another human being. And he's no agitator. A fine man. I pray for him. For all the good that does.'

'I'm sorry, Pauline…Sister Mona, sorry…'

'Pauline, Richie. My love name.'

'Pauline. Aren't you meant to believe that prayer—?'

'But your mammy, now, she's always been my favourite. I love getting her letters.'

'Oh…yes, she's newsy.'

148

Pauline swung round to face him:

'She's informed, Richie. She's an observing lady. But, God forgive me, what look-in does she get? And the girls…ah, they're nice enough, but they have him stuck in their heads.'

Richard wished he could start all this again. He felt like an actor newly arrived in a soap opera, handed episode ten without a clue about the previous nine. Pauline seemed to be acting as though he and not his mother had been her close correspondent all those years. He wanted to make the most of it and started on about what happened at Youghal…he wasn't a thug…it's just that enough is…you know, there comes a point—

A hand on his arm. 'You're right at your proper start now.' She tilted her head back. Dad's voice was vying with Cahal's now, a gleeful parrot, someone playing the feed: '*A cute hoor…hooor…have I got that right? A cute hoor having great gas…Is that—?*

The hand tightened: 'Don't stay sat up a bad corner, Richie.'

'Pauline, I wasn't expecting—'

Another voice. Aunt J outside the gate, peering, quivering. Pauline smiled at him:

'Will we go back up?'

'I think I'll head for Kelleher's. Don't suppose you're allowed…?'

The sweetest smile: 'I've a corner waiting. Ah, but we'll talk again. Sometime.' She looked about her at the whole wide world. 'Iowa, Richie. Come and get your geography right.'

First light.

...to thank you for your kind hospitality. I hope you had a lovely time in New Zealand. I slid the key under Aunt Josie's door and my sisters were—no, don't write 'in here like a dirty shirt'—*were only too happy to take over...*

Cold for July, even that early. The main street. Odd-looking, creamery lorries. Half-spaceship.

A hopeful thumb. *Office Supplies,* the van said.

'Limerick?' asked Richard.

'Ah, I'm for Athlone. I could drop ye at Thurles, you'd easy cut across from there.'

Athlone. The town with the transmitter, on all the world's radio dials. Sucking in and giving back. Zig-zag waves going who knows where? New York, Philadelphia, LA. Des Moines. Richard imagined himself zig-zagging on one, jumping to another. The rider who ditched the reins.

'Actually, Athlone will do fine.'

The van moved off.

'Do fine? Kicking about the country, is it?'

'Yes, to begin with.'

'Oh, big project, then. First time here or have ye family?'

'No family. First time. Right at the start.'

Delfigo Street

It took ten-pence pieces: a grey-bellied, ravenous meter in the sorry kitchenette. At any other time of year I needn't have bothered. The windows in the place were wide, suggesting that the builder had solved a shortage of bricks by tacking them in; the curtains were thin as muslin. Day or night in the summer, the rooms probably bulged with heat. But this was December: one of the coldest on record, so the weathermen insisted. Hence the need to keep the chipped little gas fire fed; hence the pile of ten-pence pieces on the kitchen counter, which shrank alarmingly as I made my search.

Apart from keeping the fire sweet, I had to stop and pat my pockets over and over. Typical of Dad: front door key, porch door key, flat key, no keyring. In all the time he'd lived at home, he'd never lost a single thing— not a knife, not a roll of tape, not the thinnest curl of fuse wire, none of his trade's essentials. But he was forever letting things drift apart: pens and pentops, drills and bits, washers and bolts. He knew where they were, always; but it struck me as a waste of energy, having to traipse about retrieving them when they could have easily been kept together.

Letting things drift was Dad's way, though: those words went through him like lettering through sticks of rock. As with washers, so with family—which was why he was in this gas-guzzling flat; or, more precisely, why I was there, hunting about for his Fleet Air Arm cap to take to him in hospital, courtesy of Mom, who was in her car outside.

151

Dad had given me his array of keys when I'd visited him that afternoon, along with a list of likely hiding places for the hat. He'd written it on what looked like a torn bit of bib: it was white—well, whitish—and it did resemble paper from a distance. But it had a smooth, almost plastic feel, and some of the writing was simply gouged into it, un-inked. Then, too, there was the matter of Dad's hand, which didn't aid my search. His writing was a spidery affair which had no truck with ruled lines. It was always Mom I'd gone to if a note for school was required—partly because it seemed to be Mom's province, but also because I dimly suspected that, were I to present a note from Dad, I would have been subjected to all manner of spatial and coordination tests on his behalf. Dad's writing was at home among the pragmatic demands of his trade: cable, red, 30 yds; breaker-switch, one, black; bastard files, two, BSW 435; plugs, co-ax, male-female. It was a stranger to discourse; it shunned elaboration. Regrettably, his mouth did not, which was partly what had done him out of his home. Not that he'd said much when I saw him in hospital. He was worryingly grey round the gills; even his stubble looked like blown ash.

I moved swiftly, disappointed that the bottom of the list was approaching. I'd tried 'brown kitch cubd,' a free-standing effort that relied on a side wall for support; also 'botm drawer dresser,' the only drawer that came out without sticking. As for 'wdrobe,' its side-shelves were tilted and useless, so that I instinctively fell to my knees to rummage under his shirts and trousers, cuffing aside the heavy material of his two good coats in case the cap had wedged itself between.

But I also moved swiftly because I was naturally in a race with the pile of ten-pence pieces—and even, perhaps, with the gas supply itself. For this was a winter of wildcat cuts and lingering shortages. Oil was on everyone's mind—or rather the lack of it. Television news showed folk all over Europe going about their business in fantastic contraptions: what looked like armchairs built on tricycles, horse-drawn cars—and, in one Italian case, a Vespa scooter with stabilizers and pedals. Any utility was now fair game to be shut down. It was all a far cry from the broiling summer, when Billie Jean and Jan Kodes walked off with the Wimbledon goods. A far cry, come to that, from the spring Saturday when Leeds, my favourite away team, were robbed of the Cup by a feisty Sunderland.

Apart from the gas, of course, there were the lights, which I'd had to switch on soon after arriving. They could go at any minute, too. And I didn't want to keep Mom hanging about. Petrol coupons were back. She resented any extra journeys, especially one like this. She'd muttered that his perishing fancy woman should be wasting her petrol fetching and carrying for him. But still she'd made the trip, disregarding my offer to take a bus. She wanted to stay in his picture…or have me in there as her representative.

So it was quickly on to 'tallboy, misc.' Anything more misc would have been hard to imagine. Of all the furniture there, the tallboy was the most apt symbol of Dad's departure from our lives. The drawers were stuffed any old how—clothes, papers, numberless chewed pencils and splintered rulers, the inevitable rolls of insulation tape (which seemed to breed everywhere when he was at home), a scarf here, a glove there, and single slippers pining for their mates. Going drawer by drawer, I imagined the back of his car in the same chaos nearly two years before, on Christmas Eve, when he decamped. And yet he could probably locate and match everything in the tallboy, even blindfolded. Strange that he didn't know where the Fleet Air Arm cap was. I rummaged on, trying not to see that as a marker of his ailing health.

The bottom drawer was the deepest; I'd deliberately started at the top in hopes that, when I pulled it out, I'd see the familiar peak and gold braiding winking up at me, snug and uncrushed. Instead, I was stunned to find a showcase of neatness among the debris. Packets were lined flush with each other like bars of bullion. Several had colourful wrapping: snowy trees, leaping reindeer. I was staring at presents—but surely Dad hadn't bought them all. He was on his uppers. The flat announced as much. Perhaps the fancy woman—generous in this as in much else—had paid for and even chosen them.

Then I noticed that the wrapping was loose on one or two. Easing them out, I found myself staring at familiar gloves, wallets, key cases. They were mine: mine to him, over the years. I was studying a history of Christmases, of presents I'd tucked under our fake, unassuming tree after Midnight Mass. Dad had always taken clinical care opening them: a mark of his trade, I suppose, a familiarity with handling the delicate innards of this or that appliance. And now, here they all were, intact.

154

Somehow they'd survived the chaos of his departure while Mom and I were waiting for yet another Midnight Mass to end. I pushed the drawer shut and, for a moment, stared dully at its handles. Hidden away, its contents were like an undeclared love: the kind Dad had been best at, over the years.

There was a low pop from the living room. It was time to feed the meter again. Time, too, to be going. I didn't hold out much hope for the final places on Dad's list: 'paper rack, side of telly,' 'larder left of stove,' and 'sink cupd' seemed like desperate guesses to me. Just as I got the fire going again, an engine revved outside. Glancing up, I could see the reflection of headlights cruising across the living room curtains: Mom, turning the car round, signalling that she was ready for the off. I parted the curtains and watched her car as it slid to a halt at the kerb.

In the second before they went off, her lights picked out the sign on the opposite corner: 'Delfigo Street.' Pure Dad, really—to find the only exotic name in a warren of streets called Binns and Steelyard and Tatley. When I first knew of the address, I imagined long days during which he'd doggedly hunted it down, possibly with another list to hand bearing columns of names under various headings: 'No Go,' 'Poss,' 'Good Enough,' 'Spot On.' Perhaps Delfigo reminded him of his wartime postings. To me, anyway, it had the same ring as Tunis, Gibraltar, Montevideo, places whose sights and aromas he would sometimes recall at wistful length. As I got older, I fancied that he would only be properly at home among bazaars and sand and rocky passes. My formative years had rattled like china to his rendition of *South of the Border*, a song that he seemed to regard as an article of faith rather than a dancehall standard. True, he was no further down Mexico way than he had been all of his post-war life. Still, Delfigo was good enough to be going on with: a charm of a name, warding off the realities of the street, its strays and scudding litter, its daubed walls.

All of which explained the importance of this damned cap I couldn't find. Irritation was now taking hold—partly because the search was becoming hopeless, but mainly because I could sense my mother's impatience climbing like a mist up the front of the house. I was determined, though, to do full justice to the list—even try an extra place or two, if any occurred to me. Treating the meter to another coin, I ran from the flat, down the dubious stairs to the front door. Mom saw me and leaned over the dashboard: 'Five minutes,' my spread hand pleaded into the night. Her reply was to get out of the car and point across the street to a phone kiosk. I still had a couple of coins in my hand and held them out helpfully. She shook her head, pulled out her handbag, and locked the door. I retreated, leaving her to phone the hospital and ensure that the fancy woman would be nowhere near Dad's bedside when we arrived.

As I climbed the stairs, I visualized the cap in the hope that such concentration would call it forth from wherever it was lurking. It had defined much of my life with Dad, being as natural a part of him as other men's moustaches or Brylcreem. At home, it had hung smack in the middle of the hallway pegs—amidships, he would have said, keeping the coats and scarves steady on either

156

side. I had a dim sense that, once upon a time, Mom had liked to see it around the place, reminding her as it did that her boy in navy blue had survived, had returned over the border and kept his promises to her. But things had turned sour. I could remember her asking him why the hell he'd kept it. Shouldn't he have handed it back with everything else? How many other men, long demobbed, still walked about in bits of uniform? If he wanted a memento of danger and misery (as if anyone in their right mind would), weren't his medals enough?

'Medals,' Dad would spit. 'We didn't want bloody bits of tin after the war. We wanted money.'

'Well, you should have pawned the bloody hat, then,' Mom would cry, at which Dad would retreat to the top of the garden and sit on an inverted oil drum, his coat about his shoulders, staring at the ground and stroking his chin.

Now and then, as I got older, I made cack-handed attempts to keep the peace. I'd often ferret around in his workshop, fascinated by its intimations of wizardry, by tools whose purposes remained mysterious, even after all of his explanations. One time I found a stone in a clear plastic box, weighing down a pile of sandpaper. When I asked Dad about it, he said he'd chipped it off the Rock of Gibraltar: 'A sliver of Gib,' he called it, his eyes going vacant.

'Couldn't you carry that around with you?' I ventured nervously. 'After you've pawned your cap, I mean?'

He tensed up then, and I braced myself for a rebuke—all the more terrible from Dad because it was so infrequent. But he checked himself and instead threw a shadow punch at my shoulder. His smile, when it came, was as distracted as his eyes. I can only guess, now, at the pictures in his head at that moment: importunate vendors on the streets of Tunis, maybe; the camaraderie of the mess deck; unlit bars selling rum-flavoured potions. Other fancy women—fancier by far than anything that Binns Road or Steelyard Lane could cough up. Women who were born in a place called Delfigo.

As I entered the flat, I heard giggling: not from behind the badly painted doors on the other landings, but from Paignton, ten years before. Here was the real problem with the cap, the cause of the rows and Dad's need to ponder bushes and weeds in the garden. The cap didn't stay on its peg. It appeared on his head in the most unlikely, inappropriate places. Sometimes I would imagine a cartoon scenario, with Dad walking out of the house and the cap springing onto the floor behind him, mewling its abandonment until he turned and stretched down, at which it would bowl along his arm, hop on his shoulder and take its rightful place. Paignton was notorious in all of this. Mom had gone off to scour the shops; Dad had sent me packing with money for ice-cream and the injunction to 'look about a bit, find some kids your age.' The money had been generous, enough for a double-scoop, flake and raspberry syrup. I found some kids, too: rat-faced beachcombers who wanted to part me from my treat. Haring back towards Dad, I found him in the same spot, surrounded by a trio of girls, two ponytails and a bouffant. They were giggling to beat the band, as well they might: there was the cap, far back on his head, riding his curls like a pontoon at anchor. I didn't think he'd brought it with him; I certainly didn't think it was in the beach bag he'd been swinging all morning. I thought of that cartoon caper again: it must have scuttled into the boot of the car while no one was looking.

I stopped yards from him. If I'd run straight up, though, he wouldn't have noticed. He only had eyes for them, intent on their reaction to his yarn:

'So I said, "Mr Bannerman, hard a 'port." Hadn't a clue what I meant. Fresh out of naval school, see, just a load of book learning, never been near a boat since he was a kid at Llandudno. "Hop to it, Mr Bannerman," I says. "Do you want us sharing the hardtack with Davy Jones?" So he points to starboard and looks at me, face full of hope, like I was supposed to pat him on the head and fix him up a night with Betty Grable…'

It was a good impression, I'll grant him that: all those plummy lieutenants and captains he loudly despised at home, in the pub, wherever friends or family were in earshot, were now speaking as one through his tilted mouth. At the time I was nonplussed, but I cottoned on later: here were three eyefuls—typists on a spree from Kettering or wherever; of course they liked a sailor, it was culturally decreed, but a sailor who was also a bit of posh—well, bull's-eye. Assuming this, Dad doubtless saw himself as a true son of Empire, first cousin to Monty or Tedder, perhaps, wooing three sun-kissed maidens from Delfigo with his salty knowhow.

Sadly, they were never to learn how the feckless Mr Bannerman made out. Skull and crossbones were closing in: 'Get that off your head at once, you clown,' yelled

Mom, marching up from the opposite direction. The maidens scattered, showering Paignton front with their laughter. That evening, they would no doubt regale three smirking consorts with their tale of this old geezer, probably drunk, who was parading about in some daft hat he'd filched from an arcade. Just then, I felt something cold on my hand; the remaining ice-cream, forgotten as I lurked in the shadow of John Mills, had melted from the cone. Since I went unremarked by Mom and Dad, I slipped round a nearby shelter, dumped the cone, and occupied myself by licking my hand while they traded mouthfuls until, having no garden to hand, Dad stalked off to the Maid of Devon bar.

By now I was kneeling over the paper rack, waiting for the sounds of insult and Dad's heavy tread to die away. Paignton was the worst, but there'd been other times, of course: some Christmases the cap was never back on the peg; birthdays, his and mine, would see him strolling about the house, cap on straight, inspecting fitments and furniture as though they were bunks and kit. And Mom would always brace herself when a trip to relatives was in the offing, knowing that days of loud disputation would end at some pub where there was a cabaret, knowing too that Dad would board the proceedings like a pirate and take the stage with his cap and his party turn. Once again I saw myself venturing from smelly Children's Rooms in a score of such places and staring at the tables of punters—some with hands to their ears, others looking in shock at their glasses—while Dad took them south of the border, bellowing his love of harbours, heat, the joys of an endless fiesta.

Suddenly I didn't want to find the cap, and I was glad that it wasn't in the rack, the larder, or the sink cupboard. I wanted Dad to make a new, capless start. Perhaps this stint in hospital would be a turning-point; perhaps the fancy woman would vanish back to Steelyard Lane or Binns Road, or whichever unexotic lair she'd sprung from. He didn't have to treat the garden as a place of tactical retreat. He could walk in it for enjoyment's sake, with me, with Mom. Surely all joys and contentment in life did not lie down Mexico way; surely there was still time for him to see that all fiestas end, that it is in the nature of dusky maidens to vanish like a dream.

All right, so the present was sometimes a bunting-lined port packed with cheering locals, expansiveness and booze at the ready; but sometimes it was just rainswept and vacant. Still, most folk managed to put in there, accepting that they'd have to take their chances. That other Dad, the capless one, could do the same. He might even let slip some of the love which I knew he had in him; he might surprise himself.

Again the fire went out. This time, I turned off the knob, gathered up my coat and the remaining coins from the kitchenette and went round switching off the lights. The flat door stuck badly. As I yanked it open, something bounced off my head. Looking up, I saw a high, narrow shelf which I'd never noticed, cluttered with small boxes; at my feet, winking up at me, was the shiny peak, the braiding. There was something else, too: a slip of paper, which seemed to have been dislodged from the lining. Letting the cap lie, I picked the paper up. Dad's hand, all over the place: *I formally declare and instigate*

161

proceedings for divorce. My signature (duly given). *Wife's signature* (blank). Underneath was an explanation, doubtless for Mom's benefit, that some bloke had told him that this was an acceptable way to start the process and any solicitor was bound by law to honour it.

I'd never seen such carefully composed sentences in that hand. I could have lived without them. He'd listened to too many blokes in his time, lacking the sense to leave their wisdom behind with the empties when he left the pub. And how was he going to manage this business? Was I to be removed from the hospital scene, as at Paignton—told to hunt for his paper in the day room, or tell the nurse that his radio phones had packed up (as if they'd dare, in his presence)? Or was I to sit there while he pushed the slip across the sheets into Mom's lap and waited, confident that she would instantly append her neat, sloping signature to it? Perhaps he'd want mine as well, in that same belt-and-braces spirit he used to display in his work. I pictured him lying back on his pillow, a smile broadening under the ashen fluff: just a few squiggles, and then he'd be relieved of so many years and their memories. Then the anchor could be weighed in earnest.

Suddenly the last light went out, and I laughed aloud. Despite my intentions, I'd become so concerned about the gas that I'd forgotten 'the magic,' as he called it, which was far more likely to cut out. Still, I dutifully flicked the switch; he'd instilled that much respect in me for the unseen wonder of his trade. It was something— that and the hints of a love that never quite left the shadows.

162

Up to the moment I emerged into the street, I contemplated throwing cap and paper away. There was a scrawny privet screening Mom's car from the front door; she'd never know if I stuffed them in there, and I could always nip back before Dad was discharged and deal with them properly—or find that some nosy tenant had done it already. Even as I rounded the privet, I kept them in my right hand, hoping that some saving, unconscious spasm would push them out of sight for me. As it was, I just dropped them and stared. Mom was in the passenger seat, head over the dashboard, hands clutching it, her sobs deep and almost inhuman. A couple were leaning down at the car; the woman straightened at my approach:

'We helped her back from the phone,' she said.

'Think her's had some bad news, pal,' added the man.

'Are you her—?' began the woman, completing the question with an uncertain nod.

'Son, yes,' I confirmed, quietly. They moved away slowly: 'Good night, then,' the woman said awkwardly.

Gingerly, as if I didn't quite know what it was, I rounded the car and found the driver's seat. Only when I turned the ignition did I realize that the cap and paper were still on the front path. There they could lie, I decided: the scribbled pain, the totem of times and places that had held him like a paramour in some lantern-lit dive. Delfigo was welcome to them. It owned them, after all.

First published in *The Antioch Review, Spring 2002*

About The Author

Novels

The Mercury Annual
Pilgrims at the White Horizon
(TQF / Theaker's Paperback Library)

Poetry collections

God's Machynlleth and Other Poems (Flarestack)
Port Winston Mulberry (Littlejohn and Bray)
Batman's Hill, South Staffs (Flipped Eye International)
The Girl from Midfoxfields (Black Pear Press)
Come To Pass (Oversteps Books)
Early and Late (Cairn Time Press)

Drama

Assumption Eve
FAQ
When?

Novella

Esp. Shortlisted for the UK Novella Award, 2015.

Essays and Reviews

Critical Survey, Crossroads, English, The English Review, The Explicator, Irish Studies Review, The Irish University Review, The London Magazine, Other Poetry, The Times Literary Supplement, Under the Radar, The Journal of American Haiku.

www.michaelwthomas.co.uk
The Swan Village Reporter:
http://swansreport.blogspot.co.uk/

164